Lord Cecil thinks [she would] make a lovely diversion, but he soon learns she is not quite what he expected.

Her eyes grew wide. "Do you, Lord Sutton? Do you believe in fate?"

He wasn't sure how to answer. Certainly fate—or dumb luck—played a great part in his continued success at the gaming tables. More so than his skill at cards, although he liked to tell himself he played with the brilliance befitting a son of the empire.

"I beg your pardon," she answered. "You were gentleman enough to show me to the garden out of kindness, and here I am asking for a discussion of the most serious sort."

Cecil marveled at this woman. He was unaccustomed to any member of the fairer sex asking his thoughts about life. Miss Eunice Norwood's concerns obviously reached far beyond what dress she would wear to the next party, how many invitations she received each season, how to style her hair, or how to coax the master of the house into granting an increase in her household allowance. Cecil fancied himself a man who would be offended by a woman who offered serious discussion. To his surprise, he found her refreshing.

"No, I am the one who begs your generous indulgence," he replied. "You pose a thoughtful question. One that deserves my best answer."

So, how would he answer her? What would she want to hear?

He opted for diplomacy. "I believe that the Lord used fate to bring you here tonight. I believe He wants you here in this garden, with me, on this evening."

ᴟ

TAMELA HANCOCK MURRAY shares her home in Virginia with her godly husband and their two beautiful daughters. The car is her second home as she chauffeurs her girls to their many activities related to church, school, sports, scouting, and music. She is thankful that several local Christian radio stations allow her family to spend much of their driving time in praise and worship. Tamela hopes that her stories of God-centered romance edify and entertain her sisters in Christ. Email Tamela at: Tamela@juno.com

Books by Tamela Hancock Murray

HEARTSONG PRESENTS

HP213—Picture of Love
HP408—Destinations
HP453—The Elusive Mr. Perfect
HP501—Thrill of the Hunt
HP544—A Light Among Shadows
HP568—Loveswept
HP598—More Than Friends

Don't miss out on any of our super romances. Write to us at the following address for information on our newest releases and club information.

Heartsong Presents Readers' Service
PO Box 719
Uhrichsville, OH 44683

Or visit www.heartsongpresents.com

one

Cecil, the Earl of Sutton, watched the crowd of young lords and ladies mingling in the packed ballroom of Lady Olivia Hamilton's London town house. He yawned. Such gatherings were always a bore. He only appeared to appease Olivia. He wished he could have spent the day fox hunting and the evening with a small group of his friends. Several were at the party, also appearing under duress. At least they could enjoy the comforts of fine food and drink while they commiserated.

Cecil knew the crowd. They were the usual lot. Silly young girls tried to capture attention by waving their fans, hoping to land titled husbands. The young lords flirted with sweet words and strutted like proud roosters when interested. Matrons watched and guided prospective matches, sending silent signals to their charges. Older bachelors mingled, meeting their social obligations with practiced skill. All were engaged in lively conversation, some haughty, some playful, but all with a hint of contrived sophistication. The same crowd. The same drama.

But tonight, as he stood by the fire, he eyed someone new.

"Who is that lovely creature?" Cecil asked his friend, Lord Milton Fleming.

Milton peered through the crush of people in the ballroom. "Do you mean that little country mouse who is presently conversing with Lady Evangeline?"

"Country mouse?" He studied the slim blond. "I think of her more as a butterfly."

"Really? I still think of her as Miss Eunice Norwood, Little

5

Country Mouse." He looked down his nose at the lady, then raised his eyebrows, a sure sign he didn't agree with Cecil. "Do you not see how simple her dress is when compared with the rest of the ladies' frocks? And she does not move with the style and elegance of the sophisticated ladies of London."

Milton's objections made the girl seem all the more intriguing. Cecil watched her conversing for a few seconds more. At first blush, she fit right in with the crowd. But further observation revealed that she was a touch different. Different in a charming, unaffected way.

And true, her ball dress looked like a castoff of Olivia's from the previous season. He squinted. Yes. Yes it was. He remembered the blue silk gown. Olivia had never been pleased with the way it hung on her figure. But the way it clung to the slim figure on the beautiful blond—a pocket Venus to be sure—left him wanting to learn more about her. Not wishing to stare, he struggled to take his glance away from her.

He gathered his thoughts and replied, "You seem as if you want to discourage me from making her acquaintance. Surely nothing could be further from the truth?" He sent his friend a sly smile.

Milton chuckled. "Miss Norwood is not my concern. But I thought you of all people would have been introduced to her. After all, she is Olivia's cousin."

"Olivia's cousin?" He paused, then nodded. "Ah, yes. Now that you mention it, I do recollect Olivia mentioning that her cousin would be passing through town. I just never thought she would appear on the night of the ball."

"Like Cinderella, eh?"

"Still reading fairy tales at bedtime? Milton, I thought you would have moved on to better things by now," he remarked in jest.

"More difficult tomes, perhaps," Milton said, "but I cannot

imagine a better story than the fantasy of a poor orphaned girl meeting her Prince Charming and being swept off to the palace in a magical carriage."

"The fantasy that keeps many women hoping and wishing that men such as ourselves will one day do their bidding, no doubt." Cecil chuckled.

Milton gulped down some wine. "Without such fairy tales, we might be lonely, indeed."

Cecil let out a hearty laugh at his friend's joke. "Lonely, indeed." Cecil focused on the blond and noticed that Olivia hovered near her.

Ah, Olivia! She was a vision in pink silk and lace embellishments. The new gown she had ordered to be sewn for the occasion suited her to exquisite perfection.

His gaze returned to the blond. To his discomfort, Cecil realized that Olivia didn't seem just at her peak any longer. With Miss Norwood standing beside Olivia, anyone could see that no yardage of silk or reams of intricate lace could offer a substitute for the bloom of youth.

Immediately to Olivia's right, he spied a dowager with bags under her eyes and a hooked nose. Ringlets, while appealing around a young and fair countenance, looked rather childish when framing the matron's wrinkled and powdered face. He couldn't imagine anyone cared how the grande dame was dressed. Cecil realized the woman had never left Eunice's side since she had arrived. "Apparently, Cinderella brought along her fairy godmother."

"Really? I thought the fairy godmother was supposed to stay behind during the ball," Milton noted. "But if that is the best she can look despite all her magic, I conjecture that a pumpkin, rather than a coach, will be awaiting our Cinderella long before midnight."

Cecil grinned and tried to catch a glimpse of the blond's

feet. "Shall I venture to see if our Cinderella is wearing glass slippers?"

"Only if you believe yourself to be her Prince Charming."

"As long as she stays under such watchful eyes, Miss Norwood will find herself unable to find a Prince Charming of any description."

"I must agree. By standing so close all evening, she offers her charge no latitude whatsoever." Milton studied Eunice. "Perhaps there is a reason, my boy. Do you think your country mouse might be the prettiest girl in her little parish?"

Cecil decided not to offer an opinion for fear an unwise comment could be overheard and repeated to Olivia. Eunice appeared to be more than a few years younger than Lady Olivia Hamilton, his paramour of the past five years. Even if Olivia had still been in her prime, Eunice would have offered her competition for beaux.

"I would advise you to get those thoughts out of your head now," Milton cautioned.

"What thoughts?" Cecil asked coyly.

"You know what thoughts. Any notion that you might abandon Olivia for her cousin's charms." Milton trained his eye in Olivia's direction and let his gaze roll over Olivia's buxom frame.

As he observed Milton ogling Olivia, Cecil felt no jealousy or possessiveness. The lack of emotion surprised him. "Since you fancy yourself a mind reader, perhaps you would offer to entertain us later with your talents."

"I shall save my hidden talents for my own ball." Milton sipped his brandy, watching the women over the rim of his snifter. "Our hostess may be approaching thirty, but she is still a formidable rival against any of the women here."

"Indubitably."

Milton swirled his glass in circular motions. "Tell me

something, Cecil. Why have you not made an honest woman out of Olivia?"

Cecil didn't answer right away. His long-standing relationship with Olivia was known but not acknowledged in the most formal of manners, so Milton's question came as no surprise. Why didn't he marry her, indeed? Olivia would make the perfect wife. She was accustomed to his ways. She never expressed objection to his hard drinking. For years, she had overlooked his indiscretions. And as an unrepentant sinner, he liked the arrangement. He liked it very well.

"Aren't you afraid that someone else might make Olivia a better offer than you have?" Milton asked. "Not that you have made her much of an offer."

"Are you referring to yourself, my friend?" Cecil sent him an amused smile.

"Would I betray you?" Milton protested. "No, indeed. I have plenty of choices without trespassing on a friend's. . .opportunities." To prove his point, he scanned the crowd until he caught the eye of one of the ladies. She returned his stare for only as long as propriety allowed, then batted her eyelashes and turned her head in another direction.

Milton's ability to attract the attention of any lady he chose never ceased to amaze Cecil. Then again, despite his years, Milton had maintained a trim physique and still boasted a full head of hair, albeit the color of salt and pepper. Cecil patted his growing paunch, a proud sign that he possessed a fortune that allowed him to indulge in rich food with abandon. He knew that thinning hair added years to his appearance, but he could still charm all but the most obstinate prospects.

"You are as popular today as you were in your own prime, Milton," he observed, knowing Milton's weakness for flattery would cause him to overlook the thorn among his rosy sentiment. "Perhaps I am the one who should be trespassing."

Milton took another sip of brandy. "Speaking of lost opportunities, how is Mrs. Sutton?"

Abigail.

Cecil swallowed. "Tending to the manor house quite well, thank you very much." Although Cecil was loathe to admit it, losing Abigail to his brother had come as quite a blow. But in his heart, Cecil knew that Abigail was better off without him. "I hope to return to my country estate for a hunting trip soon. Care to join me?"

"Perhaps. Maybe in the next month or so. I have too much business left here in London to depart at the moment." Milton spotted a plump but pretty young woman in the crowd and nodded. "Too much business."

"Still the rogue, I see."

Milton sent him a sly smile. "And you, the cad."

Cecil felt a light tap on his shoulder. "Oh, there you are, Cecil," Olivia said.

"Yes, my dear. Delightful of you to finally greet me."

"There, there. You know my duties as hostess preclude me from spending as much time with you this evening as I would like." She lowered her voice to a whisper. "You need to play the part of host instead of conversing with Milton all night."

Cecil was too comfortable talking easily with Milton and watching the ball from his perch. He was in no mood to obey. "In due time," he promised.

"I have two guests: my cousin and our aunt," Olivia continued as though she hadn't whispered an aside to Cecil. "I would have introduced you sooner, but she arrived just as the ball commenced." She stepped aside to reveal Eunice and her ever-present chaperone.

Studying her through the formal introductions, Cecil observed that Eunice looked even more ravishing up close than she did from a distance, a refreshing discovery. Women he admired from afar often proved, upon rigorous inspection, to possess flawed complexions, crooked teeth, or some further blemish. Not so with Miss Norwood.

"A pleasure to meet you, Lord Sutton," Eunice said in proper turn.

So as not to appear too bold, Cecil suppressed a delighted smile. On some occasions, women who appeared perfect marred their pristine images once they spoke to reveal heavily accented or grating voices. But Eunice's voice proved to be soft and refined. Everything about her was perfect. Just perfect.

He brushed his lips against the back of her wrist. "I assure you, Miss Norwood, the pleasure is entirely my own."

Milton moved closer to the threesome, forcing Olivia to introduce him as well. *"Enchantée,* Miss Norwood." He swept his lips across the back of her hand. To Cecil's pleasure, he noticed that Eunice seemed unaffected by Milton's suave gesture.

"To what auspicious event might we attribute the pleasure of your presence on this evening?" Milton asked Eunice.

Cecil clenched his teeth together behind closed lips. Whenever Milton's speech became so flowery toward a woman, he had set his mind to capturing the creature to use for his pleasure. Should history repeat itself, Milton would let her go when he tired of her, leaving the poor thing broken-hearted. An unexpected spasm struck the pit of his abdomen. Funny, he hadn't felt such emotion in a long time. Could it be—jealousy?

"I only stopped by to enjoy the ball this evening, Sir Milton," Eunice said, her voice as pleasant as a tuneful flute.

"Please. Let us dispense with such formalities. I beg of you to address me as your servant, Milton."

"Lord Milton," Olivia answered in Eunice's stead, "my cousin is on her way to the country estate she recently inherited. As much as I wish she could delay, I am afraid she will not be in the city long enough to become well acquainted with anyone."

Suddenly, Cecil began to piece together the bits of information to form a whole image. "Norwood. If I may be so bold, Miss Norwood, is Lady Olivia referring to the Norwood estate in Oxfordshire?"

"Indeed."

"Then I am pleased to inform you that we shall be neighbors." Cecil paused for an instant. "I was distressed when Sir Richard passed away. He and my father enjoyed many a hunting expedition over the years. Please accept my condolences."

"Thank you. My uncle and I were not close."

"He was not an easy man to know, Miss Norwood," Cecil conceded. "All of us in the parish will be pleased to learn we are gaining such a lovely new neighbor."

"The earl only visits the estate for the occasional hunting trip," Milton was quick to add. "He resides here in London the majority of the year."

"Yes," Olivia agreed. She shot Cecil a warning look.

"True enough, but my country estate never remains vacant and is always prepared for a sudden house party. My brother, Tedric, and his wife, Abigail, reside there throughout the year."

"Yes. I am aware of your generous arrangement with your brother's family. For you see, Abigail is one of my closest friends from school."

"You and Mrs. Sutton are friends?" Cecil asked.

"Yes, although distance has kept us from seeing each other often. Happily, that will soon change." She smiled. "And am I right in thinking that you must be Cecilia's namesake?"

"I do boast of the honor."

Eunice smiled. "She was such a beautiful infant when I last saw Abigail."

"And she is a lovely little girl, though rambunctious now that she walks quite well," he said. "Well, this is a glad coincidence. I am sure we shall be seeing one another often." Cecil caught a storm brewing in Olivia's eyes. "Although, as Milton and Miss Hamilton pointed out, I am seldom at the estate."

"Oh, I see Lord George has just arrived," Olivia told her cousin through tight lips. She swept her gaze toward the men. "If you will excuse us."

They nodded their assent before Olivia and her guests melted into the crowd.

❧

Olivia and Aunt May chatted merrily with Lord George, a development that pleased Eunice since nothing about him piqued her interest. Instead, she could smile on cue and try to make sense of the social scene she was encountering in London. For the first time, Eunice wished she had been a bit closer to her distant cousin Olivia. Perhaps if she had been, her present situation wouldn't seem so bewildering.

She watched her cousin chatting with one lord and sending a bold look toward another. Her actions reminded Eunice why her aunt had shielded her from London society until the present.

Eunice remembered Olivia's halfhearted romantic interest, Cecil. So Cecil was Abigail's brother-in-law, the cad she had often mentioned in her letters. Funny, Cecil didn't appear nearly as physically repulsive as Abigail's descriptions maintained. Certainly he was no longer quite young, but his imposing height gave him a presence and air of confidence that few other men she knew possessed. His blue eyes sparkled when he spoke to her. And his charm! No wonder her cousin Olivia found him attractive.

Eunice wondered about her future husband. What man would her heavenly Father send? A vicar, perhaps, or a landed gentleman willing to lead a quiet life of solitude, revolving around the children Eunice hoped to bear one day. A gentlewoman with but few means, Eunice suspected her inheritance of a country estate, funded by a modest fortune to maintain herself and the home's dignity, would send more potential suitors her way.

Like Milton, perhaps? She shuddered. Milton was full of flowery language, but the words pouring from his smooth tongue left her feeling slimy.

On the other hand, she doubted any serious suitor would be like Cecil. He was wealthy in material possessions, but if Olivia's reports were true, he had little patience for spiritual matters. Then again, Olivia did little to encourage Cecil toward a relationship with the Lord. No, her lively and popular cousin preferred to enjoy the company of a prominent titled gentleman outside the confines of marriage.

"I like to come and go as I please and not have to answer to anyone," Olivia had explained once. Not that Eunice was entirely without sympathy or understanding. Olivia had been responsible for the care of her mother and sister when they were ailing. Released from her daily duties only by their deaths after many long years, the lure of freedom for Olivia was great. Now that she had the liberty and the means to host lively balls, complete with a five-piece orchestra and the best food from Gunther's, she was in her element. Still, Eunice wished her cousin could find solace in God rather than in fashionable social gatherings and silly flirtations.

Eunice watched Cecil rise from his perch and lift his glass to a woman she hadn't met. If Olivia was bothered by the gesture, she hid her feelings well behind a smiling mask. Cecil had spent most of the evening stepping through the obligatory dances, eating, or standing by the fire and visiting with those who stopped by—and it seemed as if everyone at the party made time to see Cecil, even though he was not an official host. From the corner of her eye, Eunice had been noticing that Cecil's mood seemed elevated whenever a pretty woman batted her eyes at him. How could Olivia excuse such behavior?

"I see Lord Sutton is quite popular," Eunice observed at an appropriate break in the conversation.

"Agreed," Lord George said. "In fact, if I may beg your pardons, I should like to speak with him myself."

The women watched as Cecil burst into laughter with such gaiety that he threw back his head in mirth.

"Apparently he finds Sir Reginald's joke quite witty." Olivia leaned toward Eunice and said in a voice too low to be heard by anyone else, "He won't be so amused when he sees the bill for this evening's frolic."

Eunice raised her eyebrows but refrained from further comment.

Olivia tugged at Eunice's sleeve. "Come. Let us see what is so amusing."

By the time they reached the throng, Cecil was holding up a rabbit's foot for inspection. "This charm brought me luck just the other day. I won more than a hundred pounds at the gaming tables."

"Then you can afford to buy all of us a round of drinks the next time we see you at the games," Milton said.

"If you ask me to buy your ale, you must fear you will be losing your shirt, my friend." A round of robust laughter answered Cecil's observation. "But indeed, I welcome the chance to provide my friends with cheer." He lifted his glass.

"Hear! Hear!" the men responded, mimicking his gesture.

Eunice watched the men in their exchange. They looked happy, perhaps in no small part because of the effects of strong drink. But Eunice could sense unhappiness behind Cecil's facade. What could he be hiding?

≈

The supper bell rang.

"Is it midnight already?" Milton asked.

Cecil looked at the clock on the mantel. "Indeed it is. Time has passed us once again." Cecil patted his belly in anticipation. He looked about the room, watching the guests exit for the dining room. He was thankful that no one would expect to eat dinner seated, as no room in the house could hold so many people at once unless everyone stood. What a delightful dilemma. He was well aware that at least two other balls were being held in London on this night. The fact that so many people remained at Olivia's for supper showed that Olivia and he were highly ranked among their friends and acquaintances. Olivia had served him well again. He would have to think of a way to thank her.

After supper, Cecil watched to see if Eunice's chaperone would ever leave her side. To his distress, he found that the woman was like a leech—unwilling to let go unless pulled away by force. But he knew just the force necessary.

"Milton," he said, "why don't we make Miss Norwood's chaperone feel more welcome?"

His friend lifted his nose in disagreement. "Whatever for?"

"Consider it an act of charity."

"An act of charity for whom? Her chaperone or yourself?"

"You know me too well." Cecil sent him a sly smile.

"And so does Olivia."

"Olivia is my concern, not yours. In any event, I can name at least two women who consider you their concern." Cecil nodded once to his friend, knowing his planned flirtation with Eunice would be kept a secret.

"Very well. I shall use my utmost charm to distract the, ahem, lovely fairy godmother."

After watching Milton head toward the unwary chaperone,

Cecil lingered near the window. He shuddered as a wind with a bitter bite of cold blew through the gaps between the glass and wood. But before he could move away, several other guests cornered him. As they talked, Cecil peered over their shoulders. How long could Milton keep the old crone occupied? If he didn't excuse himself soon, he would never have a chance to get Eunice alone.

Finally breaking away, Cecil managed to glide through the crowd and get close enough to Eunice to tap her on the shoulder. "I see you have no refreshment. Might I procure you a glass of lemonade or cup of tea?"

"No, thank you very much. I have already enjoyed refreshments from your most delightful table. But perhaps Auntie May would like a glass—"

"No. I mean, my friend shall attend to her needs." Cecil nodded toward Milton and May. Her aunt was waving a lace fan back and forth with frantic motions and tittering like a schoolgirl, a sure reaction to Milton's considerable charm.

"Yes, I can see he is captivating, indeed." She arched her dark blond eyebrows in doubt. "My aunt is not easily fooled."

"Then she has chosen her companion for conversation wisely." He extended his crooked arm toward her. "I notice you are charmingly flushed. Might we take this moment to revive ourselves with a bit of fresh air in the garden?"

Eunice looked about her as if seeking permission from an unknown source. "I must confess, the air has become considerably heavy over the course of the ball. I had no idea one could stuff so many people into a town house, even one as grand as this."

Cecil let out a chuckle as he led Eunice through a side doorway and toward the back garden without the slightest expression of doubt or hesitation from his prey. Obviously, the little country mouse was naive enough for his conquest to be an easy one. Pity. Once the thrill of the hunt was past, the excitement would be mitigated to a great degree. Still, being well acquainted with a new and beautiful neighbor before she settled into the country would be to his benefit. He saw her first, so he could play the possessive lover should any of the other local bachelors prove to be any competition. And what a sweet arrangement—to have a new lady ensconced in the country awaiting his arrival, offering a pleasant diversion in between afternoons of hunting.

Cold air hit Cecil in the face as soon as they went outside. Eunice shivered and drew her shawl more closely around her shoulders. Cecil wanted to put his arm around her, knowing he could easily use the frigid night as an excuse, but her stiff posture made him decide against such an attempt.

He watched Eunice's gaze cut to a couple embracing in the shadows. Cecil recognized both parties. Out of discretion, he steered Eunice away from their direction toward a bench near the far left corner of the small garden. The bench benefited from the illumination, however dim, of a nearby streetlight.

"I do believe I am refreshed now. The air has done me well," Eunice said, even as she continued to follow his lead. "Perhaps we should go in. Aunt May might be worried."

"She is in good hands with Milton, I assure you. I fancy she has not a care in the world at the moment."

"Perhaps. But she does tend to worry."

"You are blessed with such a conscientious and caring relative." Cecil guided her to the bench and invited her to sit. With a reluctant motion, she agreed.

Her shiver was visible. "I should not complain, but this bench is terribly cold."

Cecil sat beside her and noticed that the chilled wood hardly offered a tired body comfort. Yet if he suggested that they stand, he feared she would desert him. "We shall be warm if we tarry but for a moment."

"I suppose." She nodded. "I do welcome the chance to sit awhile. There are so many people here. Olivia has introduced me to everyone in London, it seems. I have not had a moment to spare."

"So I noticed. You are already quite popular."

Eunice cast a modest gaze toward her knees. "They are being kind since I am Olivia's cousin, I surmise. At least, that is what Aunt May tells me."

"Your aunt must need spectacles not to see such obvious loveliness."

"Spectacles?" The sound of her gentle laughter echoed against the red brick walls of the garden. "You are too kind. My aunt tells me that modesty is a much more valuable virtue than beauty."

"And she is your maiden aunt, I presume?" He couldn't keep the sneer out of his voice.

"Yes." Her tone indicated she registered no insult. "The victim of a long-lost love. That is all she ever tells me. 'Too long ago to think about now, dear,' she always says."

"Pity." He hoped against hope that his voice didn't indicate his lack of sincerity.

If Eunice noticed the barb, her unchanged expression didn't indicate so. "My auntie is quite kind. I adore her dearly. You see, she raised me from the time when I was but an infant, after both of my parents were taken in a carriage mishap."

"Please accept my condolences."

"Thank you. I would like to say it is quite all right, but, of course, it is never quite all right to lose one's parents at such an early age. But the Lord Jesus, in His wisdom, knows best."

The Lord Jesus. He seldom appeared in Cecil's conversations outside of his obligatory attendance at church. Hearing His name spoken with such ease in everyday speech seemed odd. Cecil marveled at how Eunice seemed comfortable with whatever decision she believed He made on her behalf. Still, why would He decide to take a little girl's parents away from her? "Not every young woman would be so resigned to her fate as you purport to be."

"Perhaps I am resigned because I do not believe in the fate that you mention." Her eyes grew wide. "Do you, Lord Sutton? Do you believe in fate?"

He wasn't sure how to answer. Certainly fate—or dumb luck—played a great part in his continued success at the gaming tables. More so than his skill at cards, although he liked to tell himself he played with the brilliance befitting a son of the empire.

"I beg your pardon," she answered. "You were gentleman enough to show me to the garden out of kindness, and here I am asking for a discussion of the most serious sort."

Cecil marveled at this woman. He was unaccustomed to any member of the fairer sex asking his thoughts about life. Miss Eunice Norwood's concerns obviously reached far beyond what dress she would wear to the next party, how many invitations she received each season, how to style her hair, or how to coax the master of the house into granting an increase in her household allowance. Cecil fancied himself a man who would be offended by a woman who offered serious discussion. To his surprise, he found her refreshing.

"No, I am the one who begs your generous indulgence," he replied. "You pose a thoughtful question. One that deserves my best answer."

So, how would he answer her? What would she want to hear?

He opted for diplomacy. "I believe that the Lord used fate to bring you here tonight. I believe He wants you here in this garden, with me, on this evening."

"Oh." Her voice was soft. Her raspberry-colored mouth formed a serious line as she contemplated his answer.

At that moment, he had never seen a woman—any woman—look more appealing. He leaned toward her. If his lips touched hers, surely they would soften into a much less earnest form. He felt his eyelids become heavy as he drew closer, closer, closer. . . .

Cecil didn't know which brought him out of his dream state more rapidly—the burning sting of her openhanded blow to his cheek or the sharp sound of the slap ringing throughout the garden.

In a flash, Eunice was upright on her feet. "I beg your pardon." Her voice, so gentle only moments before, grew harsh. Before he could respond, she lifted her nose toward the night sky, turned on her heel, and hastened back to the ball.

two

Even as he rubbed his burning cheek, Cecil threw back his head and laughed. So the little country mouse possessed a degree of spirit—and innocence, too, it would seem.

"Methinks the lady misunderstood my intentions," he muttered a little too loudly in hopes that any possible witnesses would form the impression that his pride remained intact.

Suddenly, Cecil felt the chill of the air once again. Did he shiver because Eunice exited so abruptly, taking the warmth of her body—and soul—with her?

He watched a couple in the shadows break away from one another. First the lady went back into the house. The gentleman followed soon after, though not too soon.

Ah, the intrigues of romance!

Was he past all that, now that he was getting a little older? Though well beyond his third decade of life, Cecil fancied himself a handsome man, still able to charm his way into any woman's good graces. He tried to remember the last time he had been spurned. He could not.

Yet in the moment she slapped him, Eunice had shown him that perhaps he was not as gifted as he thought.

No matter. He knew someone else who was just as warm. Even warmer. Olivia. She knew of his ways. She understood him. He never spoke of how she liked to have her fun as well, a discretion that was part of their unstated agreement to tolerate each other's foibles and ramblings.

Despite the comfort he took in such thoughts, Eunice's rejection, along with her earlier mention of little Cecilia, reminded him all too clearly that he was no longer as young as he once was. His prig of a younger brother, Tedric, had managed to marry first, taking Cecil's intended to the marriage altar. Surely Abigail would provide Tedric with several sons as heirs, whereas Cecil had not done his duty to God or the empire by producing any heirs to his title.

Even Milton's query about making an honest woman of Olivia struck him. Were the powers of fate—or the wisdom of God—announcing that the time for him to take a wife had finally arrived?

If so, then marrying Olivia was the only answer. She would be the perfect wife. After the party, he would offer her a proposal of marriage. Surely she would be grateful, and his proposal would lay to rest any accusations her cousin Eunice might decide to bring about as a result of his failed flirtation. Would a man who planned to propose try to kiss another on that very same evening? Olivia would find such a notion ridiculous. No matter that he had only decided to propose well after midnight.

Olivia was sure to be overcome with joy that the moment had arrived after all these years. He anticipated her response—a quick acquiescence, a ceremony within the year, and an heir less than a year after that. He smiled to himself.

Yes, a marriage proposal was a good idea. A very good idea. He rose from the bench and headed back inside with the greatest of haste.

As he reentered, he discovered that the partygoers were leaving. Olivia was bidding the last stragglers, the couple he had seen in the garden, adieu. The musicians were packing up their instruments after a long night. Cecil realized he had lost his chance to announce their engagement that evening. No matter. The development would provide a delightful excuse for another festivity, an event sure to be as triumphant as tonight's. Judging from the ebb and flow of the crowd, the most desirable people in London had attended Olivia's ball last. Even better, Cecil could tell by their prolonged stays that some of the guests had not attended either of the other two events being held in London that night. The success of the evening reflected well upon Olivia's status as a hostess and how favorably she was regarded by London society.

After the last guests had departed, Olivia rushed toward a seat beside the dimming fire in the parlor. Though tiredness made her face appear ten years older than her twenty-nine years, a look of contentment shadowed her features with an element of rapture. She sat down and sighed.

"You deserve a rest, my dear." Cecil sat beside her. "The ball was quite a success. I offer you my congratulations. Never let it be said that you are not the most gracious and popular hostess in the city—perhaps in all the empire."

"You do speak in hyperbole tonight." Despite her small chastisement, her face reflected a glow that showed his words pleased her. She looked at the ceiling, which was just below the room where Eunice and her aunt were to sleep. "I wonder what my cousin thought about the evening's festivities. She seemed to be having a delightful time, but, suddenly, she disappeared a half hour after supper without bidding anyone a good evening." Olivia leaned closer to him. "Did you perchance notice any upset?"

He hoped Olivia didn't already know what had transpired between him and Eunice in the garden. "Why do you ask me? Surely your cousin spent the greatest portion of the evening with you and your aunt."

"Indeed." Olivia sighed. "I suppose there is no cause for alarm then."

He breathed an inward sigh of relief. Good. If anyone had noticed anything in the garden, word hadn't gotten back to her. "Surely they are both tired after such a long journey. Obviously, your aunt and cousin are enjoying a restful slumber in the comforts of the bedchamber you so graciously provided for them tonight. Such fine entertainment." He paused. "They certainly never could have enjoyed such an evening of lavishness in Dover."

"True."

"I suggest we dispense with any worries and instead end this successful and glorious night on the cheeriest of notes." Suddenly nervous, he became conscious of the crackling fire. Determined to go on, he leaned toward her and took her hands in his. He realized he liked how familiar they felt. "I have a question for you."

When she peered upon his face, her eyes narrowed just a bit. "What is it?"

"I should have asked this long ago. . .in fact, when I was young enough to consider presenting my proposal on bended knee." He took in a breath to continue.

"Proposal?" She startled, then composed herself. Her face held a look of rapt anticipation.

"Then you know what I plan to say," he said, relieved that he wouldn't have to pose the question in its entirety.

She released his hands and clapped hers together, reminding him of little Cecilia when she expected a gift. "Oh, this is too delightful," Olivia said. "Do go on."

So she wasn't going to make this any easier on him. He supposed she deserved to hear the question asked in a proper manner. After all, she'd been waiting a long time. "Olivia." He choked.

"Yes?" She cocked her head to one side and looked at him out of the corner of her eyes. Clearly, she was enjoying his discomfort. "Are you certain you wouldn't like to get on your knees?"

Afraid she might insist if he tarried, he blurted, "Olivia, will you marry me?"

She set her back flush against the chair and laughed aloud.

Irritability flowed through him. "I fail to see the humor in my proposal. My question is quite serious."

"Really?" She folded her arms. "Then is that all you have to say?"

"I cannot imagine a question much larger."

"What? No argument about how wealthy I will be or how I will finally enjoy full respectability as the lady of Sutton Manor?" she asked. "Come now, surely a man with your talent for verbosity can do better."

He puffed up his chest and cleared his throat. "I believe few words will suffice when the party to whom the question is posed is already well aware of the facts."

"So you say," she answered. "And you think I should not feel the least bit of remorse if, by accepting your offer, I would be displacing your poor brother and his wife."

He hadn't thought of that possibility. "I assure you, I will not leave my brother and his wife, and certainly not little Cecilia, without a home."

She looked about the room. "Then you expect to live here?"

Following her gaze, Cecil noted that he had well provided Olivia with the funds to supplement her existing furnishings. Italian tapestries that he had especially imported as a gift for Olivia's last birthday decorated the freshly papered wall. Tomorrow, the maids would set the Persian rugs he bought for Olivia back on the shining floors.

"Would living here be such a terrible fate?" he asked.

"I suppose not." She shrugged. "Though this is not a manor house."

"But this house is the home of your childhood, right in the center of the city you love." His eyebrows rose. "I have no recollection that you ever harbored a desire to experience the joys of country living."

Olivia twisted her mouth, a sure sign that she couldn't argue.

"And I doubt you would care to ensconce yourself in my small bachelor's room here in the city."

"I am aware of where you spend most of your time, and I assure you, I would much prefer to remain here in my own home."

He felt a victorious smile touch upon his lips. "Good. All is settled."

"No. All is not settled. My answer is no." She set her thin lips into a hard line.

Surely he had heard incorrectly. "No?"

"No." She stood up as though the motion would give her fortitude. "I am honored by your request, late though it is, but I cannot accept."

Rising from his seat as etiquette required, he tried to think of reasons why she would rebuff him. "So you have a better offer?"

"I have had many offers, but none as fine as yours," she said. "No, I simply do not wish to marry."

"What an odd thing for a woman to say."

"As you have often noted yourself, I am a most extraordinary woman."

"In many ways."

"The primary consideration is that I have the means to live as I wish, and I wish, at this time, to live in my present circumstance."

So she was rejecting him? Never in the history of his bachelorhood had he been spurned twice in the course of one evening. Cecil searched for a response but found none forthcoming. How could a spinster not wish for the utmost in respectability? She had never acted as though he repulsed her.

What was keeping her from accepting his proposal?

He searched for a ray of hope in her answer and, when he found it, reached skyward with his words. "But you do not say you will never marry me. Just not at the present time."

"I suppose I did say that."

"But I do not understand. If you are insistent upon living as you presently do, what circumstance would cause you to change your mind?"

She looked him over in the way that he had seen her study a vase or other objet d'art she contemplated purchasing. "Perhaps I might reconsider if you meet certain conditions."

Certain conditions? How dare she make demands upon him, the Earl of Sutton! Why, he would not stand for it!

Or would he?

He had to know. "What conditions? I ask only out of sheer curiosity. Do not expect me to meet your demands. I have many other eager prospects, you know."

"Indeed." Her icy tone indicated that Olivia was well aware of the juicy tidbits of gossip about him that had been a consistent source of rumor since his discovery of the pleasures of gambling, wine, cigars, and the fairer sex.

"My conditions are not small, but they will be well worth pursuing," she explained. "First, you must give up your trips to the gaming tables."

"The gaming tables? But my dear, they are a harmless diversion. And I almost always win."

"So you want me to think. Do I look like a fool? Even if you do win, I know you spend most of your winnings treating the house to a round of ale. And speaking of ale, you must drink considerably less than you do at the present time. A glass of port for dessert each night is enough for any respectable gentleman."

"Just one glass of port? How about two? Two glasses aren't

so much." He held up his thumb and forefinger and brought them an inch apart. "They hardly hold this much."

"If that were true, then five glasses would be sufficient. Which makes me believe that your port consumption should be measured in drops, not by the glass, since you can certainly procure a large glass for yourself and fill it to the brim."

No answer formed upon his lips. She knew him too well.

"Then there is the issue of your smoking. I would prefer that you not smell up yourself and my home with the stench of tobacco."

"Stench?" he protested. "Why, I buy the finest tobacco available."

She sniffed as though smelling spoiled mutton. "It all stinks."

"But I wear a smoking jacket," he pointed out.

"And yet the smell of tobacco clings to your skin and hair." She wrinkled her nose.

He swept his hand toward the fireplace. "Surely you mistake the scent of the wood burning here for my tobacco."

"Which does not explain the peculiar odor in the summer." She paused. "Also, you must improve your table manners."

He placed his hand on his chest. "But my dear, I do possess the finest in table manners. After all, I am a titled gentleman."

"You certainly do possess table manners—table manners acceptable in a tavern."

Cecil shook his head. "My dear, I had no idea you were aware of the proper etiquette employed in a tavern." He clicked his tongue to mock her.

"And finally, your eyes must rove no longer. They must be focused on me exclusively." She folded her hands at her waist and studied him. "Those are my demands."

At that moment, he wanted to throw himself on her mercy, hoping she would change her mind. How could he give up every amusement he enjoyed in life just so he could sire a legitimate heir? Many of his friends fathered broods of children by mistresses and wives alike without breaking stride. What right did she have to ask him to do otherwise?

His reasoning supplied him with the courage to challenge her. "And if I do not accept your conditions?"

"I shall call upon one of my other potential suitors to act as my unofficial host for future events."

He formed pictures in his mind of the other suitors Olivia meant. If there were others, they were the epitome of discretion. He decided to call her bluff. "Other potential suitors?"

"Lord George, for one. He was quite charmed by my conversation this evening."

"My dear, how could you make such an error? I have always considered you much too sophisticated to mistake the impeccable manners of a gentleman for a serious flirtation."

"I have made no mistake. You are correct. I am sophisticated. I can read a man very well. And I know his interest in me could be developed into something more interesting— with the first bat of my eyelashes."

"And an expensive bat that would be." He chuckled. "I have a notion as to how much I will need to settle your accounts for this evening's entertainment alone. You say you have the means to live alone, and I am well aware that you do. But entertaining on the lavish scale you desire and appearing in the elaborate silk gowns you enjoy," he said, letting his gaze sweep over her costly gown, "would consume your fortune too quickly to assure you would not live in poverty in your old age. While I can envision your devout cousin Eunice content in such circumstances, I cannot imagine a woman such as yourself finding peace and solace living with the discipline of a Spartan."

To remind her of his ability to secure luxury, he chose that moment to meander over to the liquor table so he could pour himself a large glass of forbidden brandy. He took her lack of objection as a sign that she was thinking about the life she proposed to throw away. Cecil turned toward Olivia, swirled the amber liquid in the snifter, and took a gulp as he looked at her through the glass. "So. Are you so sure your friend Lord George would be willing, or able, to fund your taste for luxury?"

"I am quite certain that Lord George has the ability to fund any luxury he desires," she protested. "Now, I ask you, am I to assume from your brazen consumption of brandy that you are not up to my challenge?"

"Up to your challenge? Are you implying that I do not have the will or the ability to change my ways if I choose?"

"I imply nothing. I only want to know if you accept. Otherwise, I will consider myself a free woman."

How dare she deliver him an ultimatum!

He had seen Olivia act in vindictive rage before. If he didn't make the attempt, she would make him the laughingstock of London. She would gossip to everyone they knew that he was too weak to so much as try to change. By the time she was through with him, everyone, including the servants, would be laughing behind his back. Besides, a man of his intellect could find ways to break her rules without really breaking them.

The love he once thought he felt for Olivia dissipated in light of her new demands. Perhaps when he was through, he would throw Olivia to that dog George.

He finished his brandy in two swallows.

"Very well. I accept your challenge. In one year, I shall return to you a changed man."

three

Eunice awoke in a large canopied bed with a soft down mattress and a warm comforter the color of gold. Why did her stomach knot in fear?

Suddenly she remembered. Olivia's devotee had tried to kiss her in the garden. While Eunice didn't regret rebuffing Cecil with a slap to the cheek, she knew the act would not be without consequences.

"Heavenly Father," she whispered, "forgive me. I pray I did nothing untoward to invite Cecil's attentions. Help me to be demure and focused on Thee. In the name of Thy Son, Jesus, amen."

How could she face her cousin? She wished she could slink out the back door, unnoticed as though she were the scullery maid, and disappear into a crowd on a back street of London. But she could not. She was a gentlewoman, a position of birth that required her to act as one.

Strong sunlight peeking through the cracks in the draperies indicated she wouldn't be able to avoid Olivia much longer. For a brief moment, she hoped she could hide behind her aunt's skirt. Brightened by the idea, she rose and rushed to the bedroom next door.

Eunice knocked, but her aunt didn't answer. She pushed the door open and peered into the dim room. A large lump underneath blue bed coverings indicated that her aunt still slept. She approached the bed and shook the sleeping figure.

"Auntie? Are you awake?"

The old woman snorted and turned over in bed.

She shook her again. "Auntie May? You should be getting up. It must be well past the breakfast hour by now."

Aunt May groaned, then answered without moving. Her voice was muffled by the covers. "Food! No food. My stomach ails me, it does."

"Perhaps fortification would make you better," Eunice prodded.

"Noon. I shall eat at the noon hour. Tell Cook to prepare leg of mutton, parsnips, and oyster soup."

"Auntie, we have no notion what they serve here. This is not Dover. We are at Olivia's, remember?"

"She has any food she wants," Auntie argued. "Let me be."

Sighing, Eunice returned to her own room, dillydallied through her morning toilette, and, for more reasons than one, took extra time with her morning prayers. Perhaps Olivia would grow impatient and begin her day without her.

Such was not to be. When she made her way downstairs much later, Eunice found Olivia sitting in the dining hall, taking her place at the head of the table.

"Ah, there you are. I was beginning to fear I would have to eat breakfast alone."

"I beg your indulgence. I meant not to delay your breakfast."

"But you did not." Olivia set her linen napkin in her lap with flourish. "I usually have it brought to me in bed, you know, but when I have guests, I partake here."

Eunice took a seat beside her cousin. "I trust my appearance here does not disappoint you, then."

"It does not. And in turn, I trust you enjoyed yourself last night," Olivia observed.

"Indeed."

"What a sluggard of a hostess you must think me," she noted without displaying an ounce of sincerity. "I fully intended to bid you good night, but you and Aunt May disappeared so soon."

"Oh, no. We fully understood that you needed to tend to your other guests, of which there were many. I do not recall ever being in such a large crowd."

"I do suppose life is different in Dover." Olivia smiled. "So did you find the ball to your liking?"

Eunice wished she could be honest. How could she tell her cousin that the man Olivia loved tried to kiss her in the garden? She searched for something, anything, to say. "The food was exquisite. I have never seen such succulent treats. The tables practically groaned in agony." She paused. "That is, until your guests descended upon them with abandon."

Olivia's laughter echoed in the dining room as she added salt to the egg in her bone china eggcup. "Yes, I am known for the food at my parties."

"I can see why." Eunice tapped her egg and removed the cap. "I am afraid Auntie overindulged." She dipped a finger of toast into the egg and took a bite of the yolk-soaked bread, eating slowly so she could savor the rich flavor. Olivia's cook had completed their plates with warm herring, potatoes, and tarts of minced meat fruit. If Olivia's cook made a habit of preparing such splendid fare, Eunice didn't wonder why all of London was eager to be invited to sup at this house. She made a mental note to eat small portions so as not to make the same error as her aunt.

"Overindulged? The poor dear. Surely now that you have come into your inheritance, both of you will soon become accustomed to the finest foods." Olivia took a sip of tea. "The finest available in the empire, that is."

"I doubt I shall instruct our cook to prepare anything so succulent for everyday fare," Eunice informed her. "We are to be stewards of the property God lends us during our short stay on earth."

"You say that now, but you will be surprised at how quickly

one's constitution will begin to require fine food once one has tasted of it."

"Then I shall keep my fare simple as always, especially for Auntie's sake."

"So her overindulgence explains her absence this morning?"

"Yes. Her stomach felt a bit sour." Then, realizing how ungrateful she must sound, Eunice added, "We are not as privileged to enjoy such delectable foods often."

"I would rather eat a tiny bite of the finest bread than a loaf of what will do for the peasant classes." Olivia stirred her tea. "Our aunt will recover soon enough."

"Indubitably. By your leave, she has requested that I instruct Cook to prepare leg of mutton, parsnips, and oyster soup for luncheon."

"For Aunt May, I will be happy to inform Cook about her wishes," Olivia agreed. "But for now, I am glad we have this time together. So now, don't be shy. Tell me what you really thought of our little gathering?"

"I thought it quite grand."

"If only you could tarry here in London, I think you would soon find a husband. You turned more than one head last night."

"You flatter me," Eunice said. "But I care not to find a husband. At least, not in London."

"So you think someone in the country would be more suitable?"

Eunice remembered the pretentiousness of most of Olivia's friends. "Perhaps."

"Ah, a simple country squire, then. Or a vicar?"

"Whomever my Father in heaven plans for me. Or perhaps no one at all."

"No one at all? I do not believe you. You are not unconventional as I am, Eunice. You would never be happy alone."

How did her cousin see right through her? Uncomfortable, Eunice paused by drinking another sip of tea. She deflected the attention to Olivia. "But you are not alone."

"If you mean I am courted by Cecil, yes. That is the rumor."

Eunice wasn't sure how to respond. Surely her cousin was sophisticated enough to know who courted her. London society, with its inability to say what it meant and its constant intrigue, was all so confusing.

"In fact," Olivia continued, "he asked me to marry him last night."

Eunice gasped. "Indeed? When?"

Olivia's cup of tea, destined for her lips, stopped midstream. "When? Does it matter?"

She hurried to find a reasonable response. "I—I thought I might have missed the announcement of your betrothal."

"No." She drank, then set her cup back into its saucer. "He asked me rather late in the evening. After supper."

After he had tried to kiss her in the garden? Whatever was the man thinking?

"I wish you all the world's happiness," Eunice managed to utter.

"Thank you. I'm sure I shall have that." She paused. "Since I told him no."

"You told him no?" Eunice wondered why Olivia could turn down a man she supposedly loved. The previous night, they had seemed companionable enough, comfortable with each other in conversation as old friends. Another thought struck her. Perhaps that was really the way their relationship had developed—into one of friendship rather than romantic love.

"Does my answer to him surprise you?"

"I admit, it does."

"And why is that? As you know, I have never been eager to marry. Why should I not wait for the best offer I can muster?

If I ever accept one at all."

"But does he love you?"

"Of course he loves me," Olivia answered without hesitation. "But I do not love him."

Olivia's admission made Eunice pity Olivia. From all appearances, she was a lively and popular London hostess. But was she happy? Eunice doubted she could be.

"Oh, I like him well enough," Olivia assured her. "He is pleasant company. But to marry him, well, that is another matter, indeed."

"If your wish is not to marry, then I am sure your decision is a wise one."

"You are a poor liar, Eunice. You think I am a fool."

Eunice remembered all too well the incident in the garden. If a man who was about to propose to a woman were to act in such a manner, then perhaps he did not love Olivia at all. "No. No, I do not believe you to be a fool."

"There is no need to distress yourself. I offered him a ray of hope. I told him I would reconsider if he will make himself into someone acceptable. Someone who can conduct himself in a way worthy of the title he holds." She leaned toward Eunice. "All his life, Cecil has been drinking, patronizing the gaming tables, and. . ." She paused. "How might I say this to suit your delicate ears? Well, he has been known to give his affections to other women." She leaned back in her chair.

Eunice had witnessed his taste for drink the previous night and had heard him boast about games of chance. She had even experienced his bold flirtations. Satan could always find useless pastimes to occupy the idle. If only Lord Cecil had a purpose in his life! Perhaps then he would find useless endeavors less entertaining.

Eunice kept her thoughts to herself and merely added, "Obstacles, to be sure."

"If he is to be my husband, he must give up all his bad habits. Then I might consider marriage." She drummed her fingertips on the chair arms and cocked her head. "Or maybe I shall not."

For the first time, Eunice felt sorry for Cecil. How could her cousin make such demands with little intention of keeping her end of the bargain? "You are thinking of not keeping your word?"

"I doubt I shall ever be faced with the decision. He told me he would make himself over in a year. I have no confidence that he can or will."

"What will you do if he succeeds?"

"The answer to that, my dear, lies squarely in the future."

❧

A few days later, the carriage pulled into the long gravel drive leading to South Hampton Manor. Eunice looked at her new home with a mixture of awe, anxiety, fear, and dread. The house was as large as she feared. How could she ever hope to make herself feel at home in such a large place? Even worse, the rumors that Uncle Eric had let the house fall into disrepair as he pursued other interests were true.

"Oh, my. We must do something about the grass and the gardens immediately," Aunt May observed. "One would think Eric would at least have kept one gardener on staff. Apparently he didn't have enough pride to keep up the outside, where all the neighbors can see."

Eunice observed the overgrown gardens. Weeds thrived among barren rose bushes. She remembered the elaborate maze where one could almost get lost on the front lawn. From the looks of the maze at present, a hapless adventurer might well meet a snake or rodent among the tall grasses.

She thought about the stipend she was allowed out of her considerable inheritance from her uncle. "It was not as though he did not possess the resources to maintain the property."

"Precisely." Her aunt let out a heavy sigh. "And I was so in hopes that we could host a ball come summer. From the looks of the place, I see no possibility for such an endeavor."

"No, we shall consider ourselves fortunate to host a small dinner party for a few intimates come Christmas."

"Christmas? Why, the holidays are nearly a year away."

"But the months shall fly like the wind, especially since we shall be busy preparing the house and the grounds."

"And prepare it well, indeed. We want to be ready to receive the finest families in the parish."

"I am not as interested in fine names as I am in fine friendships," Eunice said.

"Then you certainly need to make yourself visible among the local gentry. The only person here with whom you have corresponded with any degree of regularity is Abigail. And of course, now you have met that wretched brother-in-law of hers."

A picture of Cecil popped into Eunice's head. She hadn't mentioned the liberty Cecil tried to take with her a few nights ago in Olivia's garden. No need to worry dear Aunt May. She would only chastise herself for not chaperoning Eunice closely enough—and the resultant tightening of the reins would only serve to make Eunice's life more restrictive than it was at the present.

"Oh," Eunice said, "I am sure we shall not be seeing much of him. He spends most of his time in London, after all."

"And a good thing that is."

"In the meantime, I look forward to seeing my old childhood friends. I missed them while I was away at school."

"Never let it be said that your uncle did not do what was best for you," Aunt May observed.

Eunice didn't answer. Although from all appearances, her

uncle had spared no expense on his orphaned niece, she knew better than to think his kindness resulted from a spirit of generosity or compassion of heart. A lifelong bachelor, Eric had been simply at a loss to know how to occupy his adopted niece.

After a childhood under a series of nannies and governesses, Eunice was soon shipped off to boarding school and then finishing school on the Continent. The fine people she called classmates expected her to wear frocks suitable to her station. But her uncle's penny-pinching ways placed a low priority on ribbons, silk, lace, and bows. Her simple frocks, worn times too numerous to mention, gave her the appearance of a poor relation.

This legacy carried itself into the present. She remembered with chagrin Olivia's exclamation that her only gown was not the least bit suitable for a ball she was hosting and how her cousin had then tossed an unwanted blue frock her way. She was only grateful that no one seemed to realize she had to appear in Olivia's dress from the past season. Or at least they were kind enough not to embarrass her by mentioning the fact.

In truth, she couldn't place the entire burden of blame for her unpopularity at school on her uncle. Her penchant for solitude with her books of learning and devotion did little to endear her to frivolous classmates. She hoped that over the years her old friends hadn't become so silly. In light of her present condition, she wondered if her serious disposition would prove to be a blessing.

What was left of the household staff—the cook and two maids—greeted Eunice and May upon their arrival. They could not delay in hiring additional staff.

Memories, most of them only mildly fond, filled Eunice's mind as they toured the old house. When she left years ago, Eunice remembered flawless paint and pristine if not cheerful wallpaper. Now the walls showed that no one had bothered to keep them clean for years. Doors creaked, and evidence of mice littered each room.

"This is atrocious!" Aunt May said. "Even worse than I imagined."

"I must agree, Auntie."

"What a disgrace to our family name for this house to be in such condition." Aunt May made a clicking sound with her tongue and shook her head. "I suppose poor Eric just did not feel well enough to give this house its proper due. Why, the memories I have growing up here." She pointed to a vacant front room. "Mama and Papa always hosted grand balls and fabulous dinner parties. They were the talk of the parish. Everyone wanted an invitation to gatherings here at South Hampton. They must be turning over in their graves, God rest their souls."

"Do not worry yourself, Auntie dear. This house is only built of bricks and mortar. We can hire men to repair it, spruce it up, and bring it back to its former glory."

"I hope so. We have a lot of work to do. We'll begin in the morning."

For the first time, Eunice was almost glad the house was in such a state of disrepair. Redecorating would keep her mind off her anxiety about what might happen should she encounter Lord Sutton again.

☙

"Cecil!" Tedric greeted his brother. "So good to have you home again. I have already made arrangements for a group of us to go pheasant hunting at the end of the week."

The anticipation of such a trip filled Cecil with a cheer he hadn't felt since the night of the ball. "Very good. I knew I could count on you to provide for a great deal of my entertainment." He looked around the study as he settled into his chair. "You have the place looking especially welcoming."

"I am glad it meets with your approval. The servants have been working with diligence to see to it that the house sparkled for you." Tedric took a seat.

"I am aware that it is no small task to keep a house full of servants in order. You and Abigail have done a fine job here."

"Abigail does not surprise me. I do believe she has fallen in love with this place." He smiled. "The maid shall be in soon with your glass of port."

Cecil fought a brief moment of temptation. A glass of the strong red wine sounded so appealing at the moment. The long trip had left him tired. The older he grew, the more travel seemed to exhaust him. If he could have only one small glass of port, he would be able to fall quickly into a sound sleep. But no, he couldn't.

"Thank you all the same, but I think I shan't imbibe tonight."

"Shan't imbibe?" Tedric threw back his head and let out a pleasant but hearty laugh. "Are you sure you are my brother?"

Cecil chuckled. "Did I not tell you that I am turning over a new leaf?"

"For Olivia." Tedric nodded. "According to your last missive." He folded his arms as though convinced of Cecil's failure.

"For Olivia."

"You must be quite smitten with her to undertake such drastic changes in your lifelong habits."

"I did offer her a proposal of marriage."

"And she gave you these conditions?" Tedric sent his gaze to the ceiling and back. "Really, Cecil, if she is making those types of demands upon you, this does not sound like a sure foundation for a lifetime union. As much as I would like to see you give up your less desirable habits, can you really succeed under such conditions? If you are only trying to please her and are not changing your ways because you have found it in your heart to do so, I do not see how you can succeed."

"You do not seem to believe my constitution—or my will—is strong enough."

"I think it will be for now, but what happens after you marry? Will you revert to your old ways?" Tedric asked.

"Maybe," Cecil admitted.

"My point exactly. You are a popular man. Surely there are other women you can approach to give you an heir."

"Do you believe the production of heirs is the only reason for my decision to marry?"

Tedric didn't hesitate to answer. "Yes, I do. You have enjoyed many years of bachelorhood, and I see no other reason for you to take such a step."

"Do you object?" Cecil asked. "After all, my heir could produce a change in your own circumstances."

"I enjoy security as much as the next man, but if a change is the will of the Father in heaven, so be it. Scripture says, 'Boast not thyself of to morrow; for thou knowest not what a day may bring forth.'"

"A wise proverb, to be sure," Cecil said. "My brother, in your kind response, you have just passed my impromptu test. Regardless of how many heirs I produce, I do not anticipate a change in your living arrangement. My place in London is not suitable for a wife, but I plan to ensconce the two of us in a town house after our marriage."

"Olivia owns a home in London at present, does she not?"

Cecil cleared his throat. "Yes, she does. So you see, you have no reason to fear."

"Your heirs might not feel as generous as you do, but until they are born and old enough to object, I thank you for your consideration."

"And speaking of consideration, please do your best to keep me away from all temptations." He touched his forefingers together. "First, do not plan any events where I might be tempted to place a bet."

"Any type of bet?"

"Correct. I plan not to wager a quid on any game from now on. And in keeping with that resolution, no strong drink. I shall consume hot tea and hot tea only from this moment on." He wagged his finger at Tedric to show his determination.

"But you will indulge in the occasional cigar?"

"Olivia has expressed distaste for the aroma of fine tobacco." He shook his head. "Frankly, I will never understand women."

"Her demands have left you with a tall order. I suppose my only alternative is to keep you locked up in a room all alone with nothing to do but stare out the window and read your Bible."

"Such a plan is enough to cause a man to drink," Cecil joked. "No, that is not the solution. To be successful, I must change my ways within the context of my usual habits. I must continue to socialize, to show my friends and acquaintances that I am not a man of overindulgences. Once they realize the seriousness of the matter, they will cease to expect me to return to my old ways."

"That sounds like a wise idea," Tedric agreed.

Abigail knocked on the door of the study.

"Ah, there you are, my dear," Tedric said as he rose to greet his wife.

Cecil followed suit. "How lovely to see you again, Abigail." Abigail hadn't changed since the day she married Tedric. If anything, motherhood had made her grow more beautiful. He hoped Olivia would react in like manner once she began producing heirs for him.

"I trust your trip met with favorable conditions?"

"Yes, thank you. The weather was pleasant and I found my carriage comfortable." He motioned to the most padded chair in the study. "Please take a seat. Tedric and I have been discussing a matter of some importance to you since it involves arrangements for my comfort and discipline during my stay here."

Pained distress grew on Abigail's face as Cecil informed her of the week's developments and of his resolutions. "How will you ever change so many of your ways in such a short amount of time?" she wondered aloud. "As your relation by marriage and in the interest of your personal welfare, I beg your indulgence to speak without fear of reprisal."

Cecil braced himself for a loving but sure insult. "If I am serious about change, I must be willing to consider your frank opinion. Yes, you have my leave to speak, as long as your husband consents."

"Abigail is a wise woman whose opinion I value highly," Tedric said.

"Thank you. Cecil, you are so well known for your style of life, it has become a part of who you are. Your lavish entertainments and generosity to your friends and acquaintances are known everywhere. Those who have enjoyed your hospitality are sure to offer stiff resistance to any change."

"I agree," Tedric said. "I must add, Cecil, that perhaps you might be better off without some of the people you consider friends, particularly if they never reciprocate your generosity."

Cecil swallowed. Indeed, how many of the people he knew would fall away if he decided to change? Just as the thought entered his mind, he mentally swatted it away as if it were no more than a bothersome housefly. "Miss Hamilton has never forbid me to host parties or to buy drinks for my friends. Rather, she encourages a healthy social life."

"So I hear," Tedric muttered. He raised his voice to normal volume. "I am afraid your future wife has presented you with demands too unreasonable for any mere human to fill."

Tedric's words stung. Could Olivia have made her demands absurd in hopes that he would meet with failure, giving her the perfect excuse not to marry him? The thought sent his stomach churning.

"If Olivia believes I cannot meet her conditions, then she underestimates the sheer force of my will," Cedric declared.

"Now that, I do believe," Tedric affirmed. "I have been your brother long enough to know that once you decide on a course of action, you will permit few obstacles to stand in your way."

"Obstacles, yes. By the way, there is one matter I failed to mention," Cecil said. "Miss Hamilton has asked me to polish my manners as well."

Tedric let out a laugh that resounded throughout the study. "Cecil, I am afraid your situation has become quite hopeless."

Cecil bristled. "I beg your pardon."

"I do not mean any offense, brother, but your intended has asked you to change the very fiber of your being."

"I think the very fiber of my being is polite enough, thank you very much."

Abigail tittered. "Oh, Cecil. Do not distress yourself. Can we not all benefit from a little more polish?" She placed her hand on his arm. "I have a wonderful idea that will help you on your way. Now do not worry yourself any longer."

"What idea?"

"Yes," Tedric intervened. "I would like to know as well."

Abigail hesitated. "Let me write a letter first. As soon as I receive an answer, I will let you know." She rose from her seat, and the men followed her lead. "By your leave." She hurried out of the room as though she planned to carry out her errand that instant.

"What could she possibly have in mind?" Cecil asked Tedric.

"I wish I knew."

As Cecil suspected, Abigail was intent on performing her task then and there. She rushed to the desk in a little room in the back of the house that was set aside for her to conduct the business of running the house.

The room represented a triumph for Abigail. For years her stepmother, Griselda, had berated Abigail. She was convinced that Abigail would never be successful in managing the complexities of a manor house.

True, the household didn't run itself. Abigail was thankful for Mrs. Hawkins, the extraordinary housekeeper she hired soon after her marriage to Tedric. Mrs. Hawkins kept a good charge over the servants, but even under her close scrutiny, the staff did not conduct itself in a perfect manner. Forbidden amours occurred. Scullery maids, who were assigned the most unpleasant tasks, were forever quitting because of the grueling work or simply moving on to more prestigious positions. Servants, like all humans, suffered trials and sicknesses that interfered with their work. Though Abigail was made aware of these developments, at least the presence of Mrs. Hawkins shielded her from the need to make the problems her own.

And then there was the matter of entertaining. Tedric had the means to play the role of host often and well, a fact that brought their status in the parish to great heights. But with status came the obligation to provide guests with the best available music, food, and conversation. Strict rules about seating arrangements, if broken, could ruin a hostess for years. From the first, Abigail had passed each test. Under her tutelage, Sutton Manor had transformed itself from a gloomy place rumored to be haunted by the ghost of Tedric and Cecil's reclusive father to its true glory as the source of the most coveted invitations.

Even Griselda had to admit that Abigail had triumphed.

But Tedric's approval gave Abigail much greater happiness.

Since the hour when Abigail normally conducted business had long passed, the fire had been allowed to burn out. She shivered and, crossing her arms, rubbed her forearms with her palms. As she lit the beeswax candle, Abigail contemplated summoning a servant to relight the fire but thought better of it. Her business would not take long.

She drew out her best parchment, opened her bottle of ink, and began to write.

ð

Aunt May entered the study that Eunice now claimed. "A messenger boy just delivered this from Sutton Manor."

Eunice placed her quill back in its inkwell and took the letter from her aunt. "This is Abigail's handwriting."

"Of course it is her handwriting. Who else from the Sutton estate would be writing to you? Unless. . ."

"No, Auntie. There is no one else there but the family." She muttered under her breath. "At least, I hope Cecil isn't home."

"What was that?" Aunt May asked.

"Oh, nothing."

"Well, open the letter."

Eunice responded to her aunt's prodding by breaking the sealing wax embedded with the Sutton coat of arms. Knowing Aunt May would never be content with a retelling of the letter's contents, she read aloud:

Dear Eunice,

I trust you are getting along splendidly in your new home. You told me you were worried you might be lonely out here in a part of the country with which you are not well acquainted and with old friends now turned to strangers. If you are willing to do me a small favor, you will find that you are not lonely for long.

I am worried about Tedric's brother, Cecil. He does not know the Lord, and you would be the perfect example for him. Will you consent to come to the estate and meet him after sharing tea with me? Perhaps you might be willing to share with him some of the finer points of etiquette. Never fear that I am attempting to trap you into an unwanted match. He only plans to remain here for the duration of the year, until he can improve his general habits and demeanor in order to please the woman he wishes to marry.

I eagerly await your response.

Yours,
Abigail

Eunice let out a groan.

"What is it, dear? Abigail's suggestion sounds lovely to me. She is your best friend here. Refusing her a favor would be unwise." Aunt May set her forefinger against her chin, which had long before sunk from evidence into the flesh underneath. "I do wonder. . . ."

"Wonder?"

"Why can Abigail not teach him manners herself?"

Eunice didn't answer right away. Abigail had once been betrothed to Cecil by her father against her own wishes. In an effort to thwart the marriage, Abigail had tried to elope with a local rake who promised to meet her but instead left her standing alone in a gloomy churchyard in the middle of a rainy night. When Cecil's younger brother, Tedric, saw the distressed girl collapse, he brought her to Sutton Manor so she could recuperate from pneumonia. Cecil eventually tried to claim the right to marry Abigail, but he stepped aside when he discovered that she and Tedric had fallen in love.

Abigail had always portrayed Cecil as the greatest of gentlemen under the circumstances, but Eunice could well understand why Abigail would feel a bit awkward spending so much time with him.

Aunt May was getting impatient. "Do you think she wants you to help break the engagement Lord Sutton has with Miss Hamilton?"

"I doubt it. But even if she did, I have no intention of sending any amorous glances his way." She shuddered. "I do not wish to disappoint her, but I am simply not certain I should seek out the company of her brother-in-law."

"Certainly he cannot be so rude."

"You do not remember Cecil from the ball?"

"Of course I remember him. He was tall with blue eyes, and he stood by the fire most of the evening. He seemed a jovial sort. The type who would add life to any place he resided."

The question being, what kind of life?

"We hardly had more than a minute to converse with anyone at the ball," Auntie continued. "Except for that delightful Lord Milton, that is. He was by far the most charming man there." She took out her fan and waved it in front of her face, which was flushed with the memory.

Eunice recalled Lord Milton all too well. He remained in conversation with Cecil much of the night—except when he was flirting with the women. And flirt with Aunt May, he did. After the ball, Eunice pieced together the elements of the puzzle and could only conclude that Lord Milton offered a distraction to her aunt so Cecil could sneak her out to the garden. Couldn't her aunt, in her advanced age and wisdom, see through the wiles of such a sly man?

Perhaps not. After all, Eunice hadn't told her aunt what transpired in the garden. If she had, Auntie might not let her venture out of doors at all.

"I wonder if Lord Milton will be visiting his friend at Sutton Manor in the near future," Aunt May thought aloud.

"Far be it for me to know, Auntie."

"I suppose that to drop a hint of a question would be highly improper."

"I suppose so."

"You must think me silly. I know he is far too young for me." She sighed. "But to be flirted with again! I had forgotten what that was like. Not that I knew too much about it. I was a bit of a wallflower in my youth and not at all as pretty as you, Eunice."

"You are too kind."

"Kind, perhaps, but I speak the truth," Aunt May insisted. "I saw more than one gentleman look your way at the ball. No doubt you will be leaving me all alone soon."

"Silly goose. Of course not. No matter if I marry, I hope you will be with me always." Eunice placed Abigail's letter back in its envelope and set it on the top of her desk. She was in no mood to respond to her friend's query.

"You will be answering that today?" Aunt May's question sounded more like an edict.

Eunice shrugged, then looked up at the ceiling and around the room at the walls to remind her aunt that the house still left much to be desired. "There is still so much work to be done. I have little time to spare."

"Never you mind. I can make most of the arrangements myself. I do have a few connections, you know." Aunt May winked.

Aunt May didn't have to explain. When she set her mind to a task, it was sure to be completed with haste.

"And you are right. Abigail and I have been friends so many years. I would be loathe to disappoint her."

"Then you must respond to her now. Quickly, before the messenger boy becomes impatient and decides to leave."

Eunice jotted a quick reply to her friend. In her response, she was careful not to make any promises she didn't intend to keep.

four

Early the next week, Eunice arrived at Abigail's armed with her best resource on the finer forms of etiquette, *The Mirror of Graces,* a recent book whose author identified herself only as "A Lady of Distinction." Eunice couldn't help but wonder if the lady was a person of her acquaintance. Unwilling to waste time on speculation, she dismissed the thought. Even though she knew the most pertinent passages of the book by heart, she thought it best to be prepared should Cecil pose an unusual query.

Abigail greeted Eunice with an embrace indicative of their lifelong friendship. "You and I shall have tea in the parlor with Jane and Emily first, by your leave. You remember them, do you not?"

"Lord Henry's sisters?" Eunice reached back into her memory and recalled two adolescent girls. Both were thin, but Jane possessed a humor as sharp as her features, while Emily's demeanor was as soft as her dark curls. She wondered if they had changed much over the years. "Of course. How delightful that they shall be having tea with us."

Abigail led her to the parlor, as promised. Eunice held back a sigh tinged with envy as she beheld the small but well-appointed room. Such a pleasant place to receive guests and to enjoy tea. At the present, her manor house was so dilapidated that she could only dream of such a lovely parlor of her own.

As Eunice was introduced to the sisters, she noticed they had changed little in appearance. Emily had developed attractive curves and possessed the same soft eyes. Jane looked as prickly as ever. She wondered how they were appraising her.

Eunice sat on a comfortable seat by the fire, where tea had already been set out on a small mahogany table fashioned just for that purpose. Abigail sat across from her, with Jane and Emily on either side.

"So how did you find the estate?" Abigail asked as she began pouring.

Eunice took a biscuit from the small platter Abigail silently offered. "Aunt May was quite disappointed. She was so in hopes that we could host a gathering of our friends right away." Abigail sent her a smile that bespoke her amusement. "Why, she practically had the beeswax in hand for the servants to polish the floor."

"Poor thing." Abigail clicked her tongue against her teeth, making sympathetic noises.

"She sounds as energetic and determined as ever," Jane observed.

"Perhaps the state of the house is a blessing," Eunice said. "Aunt May needs something to do with her time. She is already finding great pleasure in redecorating."

"And procuring new furniture?" Jane ventured.

"Thankfully, we do not face that expense as well. From the looks of the house, my uncle did not care a whit about the wallpaper, but every stick of furniture in the house is polished so it glows."

"Then I look forward to seeing the place again once you are finished," Abigail said.

"Yes, I do believe that within a few months we can bring it up to its former glory."

"No doubt," Emily agreed. "I know the place can be grand once again under your stewardship."

Eunice looked up at the carved wainscoting that lined the edges of the ceiling. A carved fan in each corner drew one's eye to the ceiling, which boasted four more fans that were open, forming the pattern of a diamond. Beige and brown wallpaper with scenes of promenading couples wearing the powdered wigs that had been fashionable in the past century was obviously an addition of Abigail's.

"You should be proud of your accomplishments here," Eunice assured her friend. Jane and Emily added murmurs of agreement.

Abigail sighed and looked at the decor as though she were inspecting the home of a stranger. "I am pleased with the outcome of my efforts. I finally feel I can call this place my own."

"To its credit. Your taste is exquisite."

"As is yours. I am sure you will be pleased to entertain in your parlor once you have put your touches upon it." Abigail set down her tea. "I wonder if Cecil has any idea how blessed he is to have you as a tutor in proper manners."

"A tutor?" Jane gasped. "Whatever do you mean, Abigail?"

Abigail looked stricken, obviously regretful that she had mentioned the lessons. Error made, there was no turning back. "Eunice is to give Cecil lessons in manners."

"Whatever for?"

Abigail cleared her throat. "Because he is due to wed soon."

The sisters inhaled simultaneously. "The confirmed bachelor is to wed?" Jane asked. "Oh, that is just too rich!" Her laughter filled the room. "Do you not agree, Emily?"

Emily's eyes widened, and she twisted her mouth in an unreadable line. "I–I just hope he can find happiness with his bride."

"After all these years of confirmed bachelorhood, I know he will find great happiness as a husband. Tedric and I are so very delighted at this new development," Abigail said with too much conviction in her voice.

"And to whom is he betrothed?" Jane asked.

"Lady Olivia Hamilton."

"*The* Lady Olivia Hamilton?" Emily asked.

"There is only one Lady Olivia Hamilton," Jane assured her sister.

Emily nodded. "Then it is a good match on either side, if I may say so."

"A good bloodline, to be sure, but I had no idea that the lady had her eye on becoming a matron." Jane sniffed, then took a sip of tea. "Word from my London connections is that she is one who enjoys her freedom."

Eunice remembered her recent conversation with her cousin and squirmed. She felt obligated to come to Olivia's defense. "My cousin was confined by the need to care for her ailing parents and invalid sister for many years. Worries and care consumed most of her youthful years. Can she be blamed if she enjoys her liberty at present?"

"Pardon me, since she is your cousin," Jane said, "but I think she should be ready to sacrifice some liberty to fulfill her duty to God and country by providing heirs for a fine family such as yours."

Remembering Olivia's admission that she still wasn't sure if she planned to marry Cecil, Eunice tried not to appear as shaken by Jane's words as she felt. Was this the way everyone talked about her cousin? Rather than contemplating their words, she occupied herself with spreading strawberry jam on a biscuit with a small silver knife.

"And," she heard Abigail note, "Lady Olivia has asked that he become polished before the wedding."

Jane let out a laugh so hearty as to be nearly unladylike. "Surely you jest, Abigail. Cecil is known everywhere for his generosity of spirit to his friends."

"Regrettably, cordiality is not to be mistaken for polish," Abigail said.

"I think it is rather sweet that he is willing to work so hard to please Olivia," Eunice observed.

Three heads snapped toward Eunice, making her feel

self-conscious. She cleared her throat. "I am greatly humbled by Abigail's confidence that I can bring Lord Sutton to meet Olivia's expectations."

"No doubt he can learn much from a woman as refined as yourself, Eunice." Jane's eyes narrowed, and her mouth curved into a conspiratorial smirk. She leaned toward the center of the table. Intrigued by her body language, the others leaned closer to hear her lowered voice. "Certainly he learns nothing by cavorting with gamblers."

A queasy feeling set into Eunice's stomach. Gamblers? An image of a dark, smoky room filled with wicked, laughing mockers and drunken men calling out wagers popped into her head. Surely Cecil could have no part of that! Or could he? Was one of those fallen women actually the "poor company" Olivia had alluded to earlier? The thought left her shaken.

Father in heaven, please show Cecil Thy way.

"I commend anyone who can reform such a cad," Emily whispered. The pained expression on her face expressed both her doubts and good wishes.

"Yes, I wish you luck," Jane agreed in a whisper, and she sent an approving half-smile Eunice's way. "Although I do wonder if this idea of a maiden giving lessons of any sort to such a rake is a good idea."

"Unless he is not nearly as detestable as gossip indicates," Emily guessed.

Abigail didn't answer right away but placed her teacup in its saucer. "Perhaps I lose patience with him from time to time and pass judgment when I should not. I know that he is simply misguided. Underneath his exterior is a good soul. I am sure of it. Otherwise, I would not ask my dearest friend in the world to be in his company for long," she pointed out. "Besides, he does not know our Lord and Savior. Eunice would be the perfect example for him."

"I know the Lord, but I am far from perfect," Eunice

admitted. "I pray your confidence in me is not misplaced."

"Indeed not," Abigail said. "But you met him at Miss Hamilton's. What is your general impression?"

She searched for a diplomatic observation. "He is quite popular."

"At great expense," Abigail noted. "As Jane said, he can always be depended on to buy his friends food and drink. And believe me, his generosity has bought him a great many friends."

"He seems quite cordial."

"He can be charming enough at times, when he wants to get his way," Abigail said.

"And his appearance?" Jane prodded. "Is it pleasing to you?"

Eunice brought a portrait of Cecil, based on memory, to mind. "His appearance is not nearly so repulsive as some reported, I have to say." She glanced at Abigail.

The other women's laughter filled the parlor. "What? You do not find him to be portly and unkempt?"

"Not too portly, especially since he is taller than the average man," Eunice said. "And as for unkempt, you must remember that I have only witnessed him during the course of a formal occasion. I cannot imagine any man would not make some extraordinary effort to appear pleasing at a formal event."

"True." Abigail placed two lumps of sugar into a fresh cup of hot tea and stirred. "Tell me something. Did you notice him drinking any port that night?"

She thought for a moment. "Yes," she admitted. "He spoke a bit loudly thanks to its effects, and I wonder if no small part of his charm might have been fueled by the drink."

"That question shall be answered in due time, I'm sure," Abigail remarked. "One of Olivia's conditions was for him to stop drinking."

Eunice thought again about her cousin's confession. Her heart ached with sympathy for Cecil. She would not even be a part of Cecil's reform if she weren't convinced that the change in lifestyle would be to Cecil's benefit whether or not Olivia agreed to a marriage based more on calculated convenience than love.

And reform he certainly needed. For a moment, as they sipped tea and nibbled biscuits, Eunice wondered if she should reveal to her friends what really happened between herself and Cecil in the garden. She studied them over the rim of her cup. Abigail looked so much at peace, so full of contentment, that Eunice knew she should not shatter her mood. And she certainly had no intention of breathing a word in front of the other two!

A shot of fear lit through her as she wondered how Cecil would react to seeing her again. Obviously he knew what Abigail had done, for he had agreed to appear for the lesson at the appointed time. Surely he was not angry. She prayed not. How she wished she had possessed the courage to face him again that evening instead of running off to her bedchamber like a scared little mouse.

"So when is the first lesson?" Emily asked.

"Later this afternoon," Eunice answered.

Abigail asked, "Table manners, perhaps?"

"You wish me to begin there? But one would think that a lord would have learned table manners at his nanny's knee," Eunice observed.

"Yes, but how soon they forget when the company they keep does not know a fish fork from a soup spoon." Jane chuckled.

Eunice tried not to wrinkle her nose as she finished the last of her tea. This assignment promised to be more challenging than she had first thought.

❧

Cecil was in fine form after his hunting trip and eager to enjoy the fruits of his labors, which included bragging about his kill and his camaraderie with the other men. The hunting party would present Cook with a dozen fine pheasants. Informal banter between the four men, along with a hearty high tea served in the study, would follow.

Before he could dismount from his horse, Abigail hurried out into the entryway nearest the stables to greet them. "You are later than you promised."

"Watching the clock, my dear? So after three years of marriage, you still miss me that much?" Tedric asked half teasingly.

She threw him an enchanting smile. "Yes, darling, terribly."

When he saw his sister-in-law's reaction to Tedric's teasing, Cecil could only feel happy for them. Truly the Father in heaven had seen fit to make them a pair. Abigail never would have been the right match for him, and he knew it. But she had proven to be a fine sister-in-law.

To his surprise, Abigail turned to him. "Cecil, you must hurry."

"Hurry? For what?"

She cut her glance from side to side as if wondering whether she should continue. She lowered her voice, although not enough to keep from being overheard by the others. "Miss Norwood awaits in the parlor."

"Miss Norwood?" Cecil's friend Sir Bertram Stoke asked. "Why, I have not seen her in years, not since she went abroad to school."

"Then you would not recognize her," Abigail said. "She is hardly a girl any longer but a grown woman."

"Yes, she is. A diminutive blond. A beautiful pocket Venus," Lord Giles told Sir Bertram. The other man, happily married to Lady Jane, simply nodded.

Cecil felt an uncomfortable pang at Giles's suggestion—a surprising sensation. Why should he mind what persons Eunice saw or didn't see? She was only giving him etiquette lessons at Olivia's insistence.

Cecil wasn't sure why he ever agreed to learn etiquette from Miss Norwood. Under normal circumstances, he could blame misjudgments on too much port or ale. But he had been perfectly sober when he agreed to the lessons. Perhaps he should start drinking again. At least if he had been fortified by a good strong glass of wine, he would have possessed the courage to refuse Olivia's outlandish request.

And to think that Abigail had saddled him with Miss Norwood, of all people. Olivia's cousin. Was she a spy for Olivia? He half wondered if the lady hadn't agreed to the assignment out of spite, since her slap across his cheek left him with no uncertainty that his attentions were unwanted. Perhaps Miss Norwood would attempt to mislead him so he would err in his manners. If she thought so, she would be proven a fool. Unknown to Olivia—and apparently to Abigail and Eunice— any etiquette lessons he could take would only serve to refresh his memory of lessons learned long ago. Just because he had let his manners lapse didn't mean he had taken leave of his memories. But if he could make Abigail and Miss Norwood think he needed lessons, he could enjoy a few pleasant hours of diversion with the lovely blond.

He took comfort in the fact that Miss Norwood didn't seem to be the vengeful type. He well remembered that her unaffected innocence, so evident in her face and style, had proven more tempting than a fine meal. Which is why he tried to kiss her in the garden. If only she had let him. . .

"You must make haste in regards to your appearance," Abigail prodded Cecil. She withdrew her fan from her dress pocket and waved it in front of her nose.

"Is your gesture meant as an objection to my outdoors aroma?"

"If I may be so bold." Abigail nodded.

"Or perhaps the smell of my horse offends you." Cecil patted General on the side of the neck.

"Perhaps both," Abigail observed.

Cecil chuckled, and the others laughed with him. "So you are not fond of the smell of a man after a good hunt?"

"Perhaps Miss Norwood will be more tolerant," one of his cohorts suggested amid chortles from the others.

Cecil dismounted and, after handing the reins of his favorite steed to a stable boy, sauntered into the house. He had already decided not to take a chance that Miss Norwood would welcome the smell of the outdoors clinging to his person. He hurried up the rear steps to his quarters.

"Where is Luke when I need him?" he muttered, his voice rough with disagreeableness.

Then, noting the time according to a small clock on the fireplace mantel, he realized Luke was probably in his own quarters, enjoying his usual afternoon tea. He debated whether or not to ring the bell to summon him. He decided his valet's tea could wait and yanked on the bell with the irritation he felt.

Luke entered forthwith and bowed. "Yes, milord?"

"Help me dress for tea with Miss Norwood."

"Tea with a lady?" Luke hastened to select an appropriate afternoon suit from Cecil's wardrobe.

"Tea with a lady." Cecil peered into the mirror that hung just over the dressing table and rubbed his chin. New beard growth was evident despite a morning shave. "Fetch me my shaving implements."

"Yes, milord." Luke hastened about his errand. "This lady must be one of importance to you since you are troubling yourself so."

"Our last meeting ended on a sour note, so I am hoping to redeem myself in her eyes." He hoped he didn't appear as jittery as he felt.

"At times such as these, I wish I were not under such strict orders to withhold your port, milord. Surely you would enjoy a drop or two before meeting with the lady."

"And have her smell the forbidden fruit of the vine upon my breath?" Cecil shook his head. "The temptation you offer is great, but I think I had best not take the chance."

A few moments later, Cecil tried to ignore Luke's pitying look as he held up Cecil's vest. He could only hope the lesson would be as short and painless as possible.

&.

As soon as Eunice saw Cecil again, she remembered the night of the ball and why she had readily consented to walk with him in the garden. As was the case during their first meeting, his expressive blue eyes drew her attention first. Their boyish appeal made her smile. She held back from letting her expression become too broad so as not to appear forthright.

Cecil smiled in return, his cheeks growing wider. Was his face less sanguine than before? Yes, she decided. Perhaps he had been near the hot flames too long before, and now his complexion had returned to its lighter, more natural state.

He was dressed in a crisp suit fashioned of costly fabric that announced his membership in the aristocracy. A morning coat tailored from Bath Superfine stretched across his shoulders without a wrinkle. The suit fit his robust form well but seemed a bit looser than fashion required. Had the earl lost weight? Surely he was not ill. No, he didn't seem to be. If anything, his demeanor seemed heartier than ever.

Then she remembered Olivia's demands. If one could judge by his bearing, Cecil's health and appearance were already benefiting from lack of strong drink and tobacco. Perhaps Olivia knew what she was doing when she set conditions on her future husband.

Just as quickly, queasiness set into her stomach. No, Olivia didn't have Cecil's best interests in her heart and mind. Any positive changes that happened as a result of Cecil's alteration of habits could not be accredited to Eunice's pitiless cousin.

"How do you do, Miss Norwood? I am charmed that we .

have occasion to meet again." Cecil brushed his lips over the back of her hand, a gesture that left her feeling strangely weak.

"As am I, Lord Sutton." She retrieved her fan and waved it lightly in front of her face. Even amid his smooth gesture, she felt no qualms about being left alone in the parlor with him. Eunice wasn't sure of Abigail's whereabouts in the house, yet she didn't doubt that Abigail's ears were primed to overhear their every word.

"I offer you my utmost gratitude for agreeing to meet me here today for my first lesson," he said. "I know our last meeting did not end auspiciously, and for my behavior, I humbly beg your indulgence and pardon."

Eunice was almost sorry she had slapped him when he tried to kiss her. Did Cecil really need lessons in etiquette? "Indeed, you have my forgiveness. I only hope that my agreeableness regarding your suggestion that we promenade in the garden did not mislead you."

"No, Miss Norwood. I am afraid I was living up to my reputation."

"A reputation that you no longer need if you are to marry my cousin." Eunice hoped that her voice didn't betray her sorrow.

"Which is why we are here." A hint of sadness emanated from his eyes. "I regret that my behavior has made me unworthy of Olivia. And I find myself looking forward to changing for the better."

Eunice studied his softened features. For an instant, she could see that underneath his bravado, Cecil's heart wasn't hard. How did the world waylay a perfectly good man? A passage from the seventh chapter of Matthew popped into her head: *"Enter ye in at the strait gate: for wide is the gate, and broad is the way, that leadeth to destruction, and many there be which go in thereat: Because strait is the gate, and narrow is the way, which leadeth unto life, and few there be that find it."*

Cecil had chosen the wide path. And he had finally come to regret it.

"Perhaps it is Olivia who is unworthy of you," Eunice observed before she could stop herself.

"Indeed?" He seemed to contemplate the possibility as though it had never before occurred to him.

Eunice decided to steer the conversation to safer terrain. "Let us begin our first lesson. Abigail's maid has set up the most formal and intricate place setting possible. I am sure you shall have no trouble at all knowing what to do."

Cecil groaned. "I remember being schooled in such pretentiousness at an early age. I trust I have not forgotten everything I ever learned."

A half hour later, Eunice could see that Cecil had indeed forgotten most of those early lessons.

"What does it matter which fork I use? Do they not all have tines?"

"Yes, but the tines are shaped differently for different purposes." She picked up two forks to illustrate. "See how the tines on the fish fork appear different from those on the meat fork? Surely, you can imagine how much more easily one can consume tender and flaky fish with this fork," she said, holding up the fish fork, "rather than trying to use this on fibrous mutton."

"Perhaps if I could enjoy the food you mention, I would not have to be so imaginative," he pointed out.

She laughed despite her exasperation. How did she ever let Abigail convince her to teach Cecil any manners? Surely only frustration lay ahead for them both. But for Abigail's sake, she would stand by her promise.

"I beg your indulgence," Cecil said before she could answer. "I have had nothing to eat since the hunt, and my empty stomach rumbles. Remembering how to use these implements only reminds me of my hunger."

Eunice's heart softened in sympathy. "Then it is no wonder you are not at your best. We must have Cook bring you something from the kitchen."

"Do not bother your pretty little self for me. I shall manage until dinner. You see, I normally enjoy a fine cigar and a glass of port after a good hunt, and now that I am not permitted, I fear that my humor is not as it should be."

"On the contrary, I can see that your charm overrules your poor humor on most occasions." Eunice snapped her mouth shut as soon as the words flew out of her lips. Why had she said that?

The expression on his face brightened so much that her blunder was almost worth the embarrassment she suffered.

"I—I beg your indulgence. I did not mean to be so forthright," she explained.

"A little forthrightness can do wonders upon occasion," he answered.

The smile that covered his lips illustrated that his words were true. His temper improved considerably, and he even took his newfound knowledge to the dinner table that evening. Eunice tried not to be obvious as she watched him, but she noticed no errors.

The lesson had been a success! She held back a victorious smile. She felt certain that Abigail and Tedric noticed, too. Abigail gave her encouraging looks from time to time as the meal progressed. She was grateful she hadn't disappointed her friend.

Or is it Cecil you wish not to disappoint?

The idea took her by surprise. Eunice had no romantic intentions toward Cecil. So why did her heart beat faster on those occasions when he drew near to her? When she caught a whiff of his bay rum shaving lotion, why did she want to lean even closer to him?

Jane's crisp voice interrupted her musings. "Cecil, do you

have any news from London?"

"I did receive a missive in yesterday's post."

"Do tell!" Emily urged. "We are always eager to hear news from London."

Obviously enjoying his role as the center of attention, Cecil reported on each friend and acquaintance.

"And Lady Olivia?" Jane prodded. "I understand her recent ball was quite a success."

"Yes, it was. In spite of the fact that her ball coincided with two other events, the crowd was considerable." He cocked his head like a rooster drawing all the attention of the hens. "Olivia was pleased."

Olivia. Mention of her cousin hadn't bothered Eunice until she heard it pass through his lips. Somehow his speaking of her, even in such a casual context, sent a wave of jealousy through her that she hadn't known herself capable of feeling. Though the emotion caused her to feel alive by showing her that she had begun to care about him, she found herself not entirely comfortable with such passion.

æ

Cecil tried to divert the conversation from Olivia as soon as he could. Suddenly, he didn't want to talk about Olivia when Eunice was present.

Eunice? What an odd thought. No, her presence wasn't the reason. Surely everyone in the dinner party found his recent commitment a source of curiosity and amusement. Yes, that was the reason for his reticence. They would just have to wait to have their wonder satisfied.

He looked over at Eunice. She was even more beautiful than she had been on the night of the ball. Her own fashionable clothing suited her small frame better than Olivia's thoughtless castoff. Soft blond curls surrounded healthy cheeks that drew the eye to her mouth, which reminded him of a sweet pink rosebud. Her expression was unreadable. She seemed far away, lost in a world of her own. And no wonder. Surely all the talk about people in London she neither knew nor cared about bored Eunice. He wished he could be alone with her, to converse with her further in matters of mutual interest. He wanted to entertain her, to make her fill the room with her tinkling laugh.

What has come over me? I haven't felt like this since. . .since. . . He tried to remember. Yes, since the bloom of his first love.

As the others conversed, he meditated. Olivia would be the ideal match, but he felt different around Eunice. He looked at the lovely blond, the diminutive woman Giles persisted in calling a "pocket Venus."

Why did he find himself reacting to Eunice so suddenly? Was it because, like Abigail, she seemed so much more pure? How could Eunice be both sophisticated and innocent?

He cut his stare to Tedric's friend, Lord Giles. The dark-haired man had been boring his stare into Eunice all evening. Obviously, he, too, had taken special notice of how Eunice's quiet charm took over any room she entered. Surely Giles had set his sights on Eunice.

A sense of outrage filled Cecil—an emotion he knew he had no right to feel toward Eunice. Olivia had her flirtations, but her actions never bothered him. The passion he felt struck fear in his heart. Olivia, and the familiar warm emotion she stirred in him, felt comfortable and good. This passion toward Eunice was strangely deeper. How could this be? Such feelings promised to be nothing but trouble.

five

"Lord Snob, shake hands with Sir Inferior," Cecil said during his imaginary introduction.

Eunice let out an exasperated breath. "Cecil, please! Why are you ordering Lord Snob to shake hands? Do you not know better?"

"All right." He cleared his throat. "Lord Snob, I know you really have no desire to shake hands with Sir Inferior. He is one of the many others that your paramour is seeing in secret, and this entire introduction is quite awkward. I am so sorry you have to pretend that you have no idea you are being played for a fool, old boy. I suggest that we retire to the drawing room for a glass of port."

"Cecil!" Eunice laughed in spite of herself.

Over the past weeks, Eunice had begun to anticipate rather than to dread her lessons with Cecil. He had proven to be a quick and willing student. Even during their most frustrating moments, he managed to charm her. His charisma took her by surprise. With his abrupt cessation from strong drink and cigars, she had expected him to be grumpy. Since their renewed acquaintance, she had never caught a whiff of port or brandy on his breath, and the stale smell of tobacco was never upon him—a fact she found even more pleasing. She couldn't help but think that his success was due in no small part to her petitions for him with the Lord. Yet in light of his indifferent attitude toward God, she would not admit to Cecil that she was praying for him. At least not yet.

As her affection for Cecil grew, Eunice felt a twinge of guilt now and again about her cousin. Was she right to harbor feelings for him? Not that her feelings mattered; as soon as he had broken his bad habits, she would be sending him back to London a changed man—and back into Olivia's arms. Olivia, the fiancée he rarely mentioned but for whom Eunice prayed each night.

Weeks ago, soon after she had arrived at the manor house, Eunice had written a newsy missive to her cousin to express appreciation for her hospitality during her brief stay in London. Olivia never replied. This omission didn't come as a surprise. Olivia had never taken the slightest notice of Eunice since their girlhood. Why should a one-night stay in London alter that?

Still, did she not owe Olivia some consideration? After all, the woman was a distant cousin.

What am I thinking? How prideful I am, even to think myself a threat of any sort to Olivia. Or that I would want to be. She uttered a quick prayer for help in tempering her pride and putting to death her growing fondness for Cecil.

❧

An hour later, Eunice and Cecil were still in the parlor, where their lessons always took place. They sat at the same table where Eunice and Abigail took tea each afternoon.

Reaching across the small table, Eunice handed Cecil a cup of the hot liquid. His fingers brushed against hers. Pleasantly taken aback by his strong, warm touch, her hand shook just enough to disrupt the cup and saucer. Not a drop was spilled. "I beg your pardon."

"Likewise," he said quickly, as though he were equally taken aback.

Cecil looked into her face. He seemed to study it, as though trying to form a mental picture of her features that he could visualize at will. She took note of his features. Even though she had met with him on many occasions, she studied his face as though she were regarding it for the first time.

Why hadn't she noticed the straight, aristocratic line of his nose before? Perhaps his strong cheekbones had just begun to appear as he shed pounds along with his bad habits. His complexion was less sanguine than before. The light in his eyes, though promising gladness, did not hold as much mischief as when she first met him. Mesmerized, she stared into his blue eyes. Eunice wished she could freeze the moment forever.

As soon as he set the cup down, he took her hands into his. She wanted to protest his boldness, but no voice would leave her lips. She wanted to jerk her hands out of his, but they refused to move.

"Eunice," he said, "you are the loveliest creature I have ever seen."

Her heart beat with pleasure. She tried to form her expression into a mask of disinterest but knew she failed miserably. Cloistered at school, Eunice had known few flirtations and was not accustomed to empty talk. Still, she tried not to become too enchanted by his flattery. With Cecil's reputation as a man of the world, she wondered if he were toying with her. A second attempt to remove her hands from his was successful, although she didn't move them away in an abrupt manner.

She fought her own vanity so she could summon the courage to deliver an admonishment. "I must remind you that though your words are pleasant to the ear, scripture looks upon flatterers with a jaundiced eye."

She was surprised when his expression reflected genuine hurt. "I do not flatter you. My compliment is sincere. You are different from the women I know in London. You possess something I haven't seen in anyone. Your sense of peace and your radiance surpass even Abigail's."

"Then surely you have surpassed Lord Milton in your flowery speech." Nevertheless, as they continued the lesson, she knew his words would always stay with her. Yet she was bothered by the blank expression that came over his face when she referred to scripture.

"Do you read with any regularity?" she asked.

He shrugged. "The newspaper. And my mail."

Cecil's bored expression told her that he knew Eunice had returned to her role as teacher and that she would have to tread lightly. "But why not read books as well? Familiarity with great literature is part of any gentleman's education."

"I thought you were instructed to polish my manners. Literature was never mentioned."

"I have seen your library. How can you possess so many books yet never have any desire to read?"

"My tutors forced me to read when I was a schoolboy. Since my release from studies, I have not perused a book." He gazed upon the draperies, although his eyes seemed to glaze over like so much frost on a window. "My father spent many years and a large sum of money in building a fine collection of books. In his later years, they proved to be his only escape from the house. I have no desire to be a recluse. Perhaps that is another reason why I am reticent to engage in books."

"Reading books does not make one a recluse." She paused. "Especially not a man such as yourself who remains fully engaged in life."

He nodded. "You have a point. But hunting is so much more sporting."

"True. But surely you cannot fill every hour of the day with sport." She regretted her words as soon as she uttered them. Cecil's past was nothing if not a record of how a gentleman of leisure could spend the hours in idle play.

If Cecil recognized the irony in Eunice's comment, he pretended not to notice. "I suppose I should venture into the library now and again."

"How long has it been?"

He shifted in his seat. "I spend most of my time in

London, as you well know. The few times I am here in the country, I am loathe to sit by the fire with a book."

"You haven't set foot in the library in years, then." She made sure to keep any judgmental tone out of her voice.

"Years. I regret that I must admit you are correct." He shifted back to his original position.

So he hadn't read a book in years. She wondered how many years but decided not to ask. She had embarrassed Cecil enough for one day. No wonder any knowledge of the Bible he had beyond, perhaps, the Ten Commandments had long been forgotten. She watched the spiritually starved man. If only he were not so proud! She knew that pride kept him from admitting he needed God. A man of obvious intelligence, he was too crafty to let her trick him into reading the Bible. Besides, according to her reading of scripture, the Lord wanted souls to come to Him willingly, not by coercion.

Eunice said a quick prayer for guidance, then she spoke. "I have a splendid idea. Why not start today?"

He let out an irritated sigh. "Why did I know you would say that? If I could be so accurate in reading thoughts on a consistent basis, I could make my money playing parlor tricks in the theatre."

"I cannot imagine such an occupation would offer you happiness for long." She rose to her feet.

He followed suit.

"Good," she said. "I am glad to see that your reflexes are improving."

"As long as you don't bob up and down too frequently. This etiquette business can be hard on a man's knees."

"You are not as feeble as all that."

"Hardly." He puffed out his chest. "But why do you rise? Surely we are not done here."

"No, but I thought we might venture into the library. I might like to take a look at more of your books myself. Uncle

Eric's library is mainly composed of dry business journals. I have already read most of the works of fiction he owned."

"I am pleased that the Sutton library can be of interest to you. But I am not sure I care to select a volume for my own reading pleasure just now," he said.

"Are you sure? Perhaps a trip to the library will change your mind." She had a thought. "I know you have a wonderful collection of Shakespeare's works. Why not begin with reading one of his plays?"

"Shakespeare." He pursed his lips. "I have not sat down to read the Bard since my school days."

"You might appreciate his wit more now."

"Perhaps I would." He hesitated only for a moment, then nodded. "Very well."

"Excellent." She began walking toward the door. He took her by the elbow and kept her moderate pace. Although the gesture was unnecessary, she felt protected. The feeling was not unpleasant.

"To read or not to read. That is the question," he proclaimed.

She laughed at his twisting of *Hamlet*. "I say that to read is to be."

"Very good!" He smiled and chuckled. "I like a woman who has a way with words."

His compliment, though quipped over an insignificant exchange, pleased her.

A moment later, they entered the library just down the great hall. Cecil headed toward the south wall. He reached up and selected a copy of *Hamlet*, reaching it easily thanks to his significant physical stature. He opened the leather-bound book and looked inside.

"Are you certain you have not visited the library lately? You went right to the book you wanted."

He looked up from his book and twisted his mouth in a sardonic grin. "My father was nothing if not predictable. The order of volumes in this library has never changed in my memory. Only when new volumes were added did Father disrupt the stability of his collection."

Eunice surveyed the massive assemblage of books. "No doubt such keen organization makes every book easier to find."

"Indubitably." He snapped the book shut. "I never thought I would say this, but I want to thank you for bringing me here. Indeed, I believe I will actually look forward to retiring early with this book tonight."

"Splendid." She said yet another silent prayer before she made her next venture. "I look forward to reading each night, too. But even the finest fiction is not enough for me."

His eyebrows formed two doubtful arches. "Are you telling me that you plan to tackle your uncle's business journals?"

She laughed. "Uncle Eric may have memorized most of them, but not I. No, the nonfiction I read is contained in scripture. I read a little each evening. I am also in the habit of consulting scripture when I wake up each morning, even before my feet touch the floor. I find the readings an inspiring way to begin my day, allowing me to focus on God."

"And does your reading also offer an excuse to remain in bed a bit longer?"

Uttered by anyone else, the comment would have insulted Eunice. But by this time, she was accustomed to his style of wit. "A benefit on some days, perhaps. If I am tempted in such a way, I consult the verses in Proverbs warning against laziness."

"A grand idea." He chuckled. "But to stay in bed even a few moments longer—for that, even I might read scripture." The sardonic grin returned.

"Then why not?"

"Even if my motives are less than pure?"

"Even if your motives are less than pure. Your admission of that is a good start," she assured him. "In any event, once you start seeking the Lord, you will be awed by how He will turn your heart to Him."

"You are amazing." His voice was soft.

"Amazing? Me? Oh, no." Her modesty was not false. Her surprise at his observation was genuine.

"I think you are. No matter what I say or do, you accept me for who I am."

"Yes, I do. For the man you are now and the man you are destined to become."

"You have more faith in me than I do in myself."

"Perhaps your own faith can be girded by your reading," Eunice said. "I suggest you start with Psalms, Proverbs, and the Gospels."

"Very well. I understand that a gentleman is always a student. Olivia should be pleased."

"Yes. Yes, she should." Eunice felt a lump form in her throat. She stood up, and Cecil followed suit. "I–I shall be taking my leave of you now," she said. "Shakespeare left quite a body of work. Reading all of it will take quite some time."

She wished he would stop her from leaving the parlor, but he did not. She turned her head quickly away from him and wiped a tear from her eyes.

&

Cecil opened his Bible—for the first time in memory since his boyhood—with a feeling of trepidation and dread. He remembered the scriptures to be a dry listing of *shalt*s and *shalt not*s, along with reports of long-ago battles between the Hebrews and their enemies. When he first turned the pages of the book, in his mind he could see a picture of his old schoolmaster. Master Evans had insisted that he learn the Bible, forcing him to memorize verses that were forgotten as soon as the lesson was completed. Granted, Tedric had devoured the tenets of the faith when he was a small child. The study of scripture was his favorite course of learning, a fact he readily admitted.

Cecil even remembered how a little glow emanated from his brother's face whenever Tedric talked about the Bible. Not so with Cecil. At least, not then.

But this time, when he looked at the passages that Eunice suggested, Cecil found it much more fascinating than he remembered. Now well past the brink of manhood, he was ready for the Word. Because of his experience, he could see the wisdom of Proverbs and feel David's emotion expressed in Psalms. Without realizing he had passed the requirements of the initial assignment from Eunice, Cecil explored several passages of the New Testament he had long forgotten. Many of Jesus' teachings that had gone in one ear and out the other when he was a child seemed pertinent to his current situation.

Not that everything Jesus had to say comforted him; rather, conviction concerning his own sin arose in many passages. Yet the offer of hope—of true salvation being possible even for a cad such as himself—gave him an optimism he had not felt in years. He wanted to read more, but the small bit of twilight still shining through the window and the dying embers of the fire showed that the day was passing rapidly. Tomorrow he could pursue his reading further. He shut the book and held it in his lap for a moment, not wishing for his time of solitude to end.

He heard the hinges on the study door squeak as someone entered. Cecil looked up and saw his brother. Tedric's eyes were wide as though he had seen a haunting spirit.

"Cecil! What are you reading?"

"Certainly the same book you read yourself on a daily basis."

Tedric surveyed the volume sitting in Cecil's lap. "I recognize it." He shook his head.

"Why do you seem so shocked?" Cecil couldn't resist jesting. "Did you think I devote all my time to reading the political columns?"

"A great deal of it, to be sure," Tedric quipped. "I beg your pardon, but I am shocked to find you reading any book at all, much less, much less—"

"The Bible." Cecil chuckled. "I know. So that you do not succumb completely to apoplexy, rest assured that I have also spent considerable time with the Bard today."

"I never fancied you would spend time with Shakespeare."

"Oh, but I am. Under duress. And I am only reading scripture as part of my course of study with Eunice. She insists, you know. She says that reading is part of my education."

The light of excitement and his amused grin fell from Tedric's face. His disappointment that Cecil hadn't given himself over to the Lord then and there was reward enough for the time being. Cecil was glad he wasn't as dull as his prig of a brother. As dull as an old country vicar, undoubtedly. As much as he wanted to embrace the Savior, Cecil dreaded the thought of losing his sense of adventure and playfulness.

Yet Tedric was married to Abigail, and Cecil was trying to change for a fiancée whose love he had begun to question. The irony did not escape him. Perhaps he himself, not his prig of a brother, Tedric, was the fool.

Tedric recovered enough to joke. "Forgotten everything Master Evans taught us, eh?"

"Not entirely. But the years have dimmed my memory enough that a refresher is in order."

"I trust you are enjoying your task, then."

"To an extent." He cast a warning look Tedric's way. "But do not suppose that my goal is to become as devout as you are. I am only doing this to please Eunice—and Olivia," he added with haste. He hoped Tedric wouldn't notice his blunder.

No such luck. "To please Eunice?"

"And Olivia. Just as I said."

"I see. I suppose the lessons with Eunice will be ending soon. After all, there are only so many manners to be learned, even by an ambassador, to be sure."

The thought of not seeing Eunice on a regular basis was an unhappy one, a development he didn't wish to contemplate. True, the lessons were becoming thinner. Vanity allowed him to believe that Eunice was finding new manners for him to learn so that they could see each other. At least, he hoped so.

∂a

Eunice tried not to think about Cecil or about Olivia. Instead, she occupied her time with the house. Selecting colors of paint for various rooms, new wallpaper, and fabric for fresh draperies cheered her spirit. The anticipation of the house, now drab and gray, being decorated to look as if Eunice herself lived there gave her something to anticipate—a process not laden with guilt or care.

Seeing her aunt come alive during the course of decorating the house rejuvenated her soul. "The wallpaper in the parlor is coming along nicely." Aunt May clasped her hands in rapture. "Perhaps we will be ready for a soiree by Christmastide after all."

Eunice remembered the botanical pattern they had chosen and visualized the motif of pink and red roses against a creamy background. "The parlor should benefit greatly from such improvement. I look forward to entertaining our friends amid such beauty."

"As do I." Aunt May smiled. "Oh, and I wanted to mention the dining hall. Do you favor that the walls be painted copper green, or do you prefer another pattern of botanical paper?"

"I think the botanical would offer a pleasing extension of the decorations in the parlor." Eunice thought about the way the appearance of each room was taking shape and allowed herself a satisfied smile. "I do believe that one day soon I shall be able to think of this place not as Uncle Eric's house but as my own."

"That is a pleasing notion." Aunt May looked around the drawing room, where they were relaxing for the evening. "Have you given any thought to our guest list?"

"But I didn't think we were ready yet."

"Oh, we are not ready yet. But we shall be soon." She paused. "I was thinking that I would like to include that nice gentleman Brigadier General Tarkington."

"But we hardly know the brigadier general," Eunice pointed out.

"Well, perhaps we have not known him for years as we have our other friends, but my dear, he is, after all, a brigadier general."

"And, naturally, you consider him someone we would not want to put off in any way."

"What is to put him off? Our home will be ready soon, and our friends are pleasant enough."

"Yes." *But is Cecil ready?*

Eunice decided not to mention her plans to her aunt. She hoped to introduce the new Cecil to their friends at the soiree. She had no intention of issuing invitations to any event at the manor house until she was certain he was ready.

She wished she could hurry him through the paces. But Cecil was no longer at the Sutton estate. He had gone to London on business, and she missed him beyond her capacity of expression.

She wondered about his business. As much as the thought pained her, surely his errands included Olivia.

❧

The carriage pulled in front of a familiar residence at the London address Cecil gave to the driver. He looked out and viewed the three-story clapboard house where Lizzie resided. As usual for this time of evening, light shone from every window. The illumination caused the surrounding yard to appear as at daylight, making the cold night seem a little warmer.

He missed Olivia. But since he had arrived in London, Cecil had felt the pull of Lizzie's charms. The bold redhead would provide pleasant company for the evening. What harm would come of his visiting an old friend?

So here he was. He tried to lift his foot to begin his exit, but it wouldn't do his bidding. No physical ailment was the cause of his inertia; his heart forbade movement. Where was his desire to join the party? He knew that many willing women awaited. Against a backdrop of lively music, they would bring him a warm bowl of pea soup to ward off the chill of night and a round of stout ale to smooth the tongue. They never minded the smell of smoke. On the contrary, all the women at Lizzie's savored the smell of a fine cigar, whether the aroma from the smoke wafted through the air or the taste lingered upon his lips.

After his refreshment, Cecil would be welcome to join the other men at the gaming tables. Lizzie would bring him red wine from an endless bottle. Rather than curtail or even count the number of glasses he consumed, she would insist he take a goodly portion. He was no fool. He knew that his lady friend took a portion of the money from his losses. She was eager to enjoy a handsome profit as his grip on common sense and prudence became weaker with each drop. But didn't amusement always carry a price? If Eunice were there, she would be sure to ask if the price he paid was too high.

Eunice. An unwelcome image of his beautiful taskmistress waxed into his mind. He had been dutiful in his assigned reading, so Proverbs 20:1 entered his mind: *"Wine is a mocker, strong drink is raging: and whosoever is deceived thereby is not wise."*

Too true! His consumption of wine had resulted in unwise decisions more than once.

Unwelcome and unbidden, Proverbs 5:3 followed in close succession: *"For the lips of a strange woman drop as an honeycomb, and her mouth is smoother than oil."*

How well the image described Lizzie! He liked to think that she missed him in his absence. He stared at the house again. Judging from the sounds of loud voices and music floating out from the building, he knew in his heart that she missed his money more than anything else. Perhaps not even that. Plenty of other men were happy to take his place and to pay her well for the privilege.

He couldn't help but compare the brash, redheaded woman to Eunice. Over time, he had come to enjoy the talks with Eunice. Her mind was sharp and interested in matters of import. No thought-provoking exchanges would ever occur at Lizzie's. If he were to ask her opinion about any of the classics, she would look puzzled, then laugh in his face to disguise her ignorance. Not that she could be blamed. Lizzie never had the advantage of being born a lady. But though she was kind of heart, Cecil had a notion that no aristocratic title could change her into a lady of refinement.

Eunice would have been refined even if she had been born to a charwoman. He remembered Giles's reference to his petite blond, a pocket Venus. Such a vulgar designation made his blood boil now that he had deepened his acquaintance with her. Eunice was modest, pure, and proper. More like an angel than a pagan goddess. And she was as sweet of character as she was of face. Eunice never expected payment of any kind from him. Not love, not marriage, not even his friendship.

At that moment, he realized that Eunice dispensed far more patience and kindness than he deserved. He was not honoring her—or Olivia—to pause his coach in front of Lizzie's.

"We are here, sir," the driver reminded him. "Unless this is not the proper address."

He paused only for a moment. "No, driver. This is not the proper address. I have somewhere else to go." When he gave the driver Olivia's house number, a sense of relief flooded him.

He had passed the first test in London.

six

Cecil knocked on the door. In keeping with his promise, he hadn't seen Olivia in months. Certainly his visit would catch her unaware. The surprise would be a pleasant one, he hoped.

"Milady will see you shortly, milord," the maid informed Cecil. "Would you care to wait in the parlor?"

"Certainly." He handed her his coat and hat. "She shall not keep me waiting long, I trust."

"Oh, no, milord."

He followed her a few steps into the parlor.

"May I pour you a glass of port?" she offered.

Cecil knew that Olivia had instructed her to suggest that he partake. Surely Olivia realized he would see through such a transparent test. "No, thank you."

"Oh!" The maid's eyebrows shot up. "We have brandy, if it be more to your likin', milord."

The brandy sounded good. But he couldn't accept. "No."

She persisted. "A mug of ale?"

"No. But if you insist on my partaking of refreshment, I would desire a cup of tea."

She curtsied. "Yes, milord."

After the maid exited, he settled into his favorite chair and wondered whether the maid had offered him three types of alcoholic beverages on her own because she considered making such offers her duty or if Olivia had encouraged her to prod enough for him to give in to temptation. He hoped the answer was the former.

He looked around at the familiar place, Olivia's childhood home that was now rightfully hers. Alone in the silence, he realized that he longed for the approval of such a strong, independent woman. Surely Olivia would be delighted to see him and express great pleasure over his obvious progress.

He waited, his anticipation waning with each passing moment.

The temperature in the room was dropping with the progression of night. Dying embers in the fire offered little warmth. Olivia was certain to dawdle, leaving him in a chilly room indefinitely. When would that maid be in with the tea?

Olivia breezed in a few moments later, sooner than he anticipated but after the maid had brought the tea. He rose to greet her, but she made no move toward him.

"Cecil!" she scolded. "If you had told me you were planning to be in London, I would have had Cook prepare dinner for you. Or have you already eaten?"

"Yes. I concluded my business with my solicitor, and we had a quick meal at the inn."

Her face lifted an inch, indicating fresh and keen interest. She took the seat across from him. "I trust your business went well?"

"Yes," he answered as he sat down. "And it has nothing to do with you, my dear. We were just conducting my quarterly review of investments."

"Profitable, I hope."

"Profitable. But you need not concern yourself with such matters."

"So your business affects me not in the least?" she prodded.

"Did I not just tell you that, or am I walking in a dream state? I wonder, my dear, why you doubt me."

"I thought perhaps you were making some sort of arrangements regarding our betrothal."

"Perhaps you were hoping I would arrange for you to have a generous allowance?"

"I beg your pardon! You know perfectly well that I can take care of myself, if I choose. I was merely planning to caution you that you need not go to such lengths unless—I mean, until the banns are read."

Unless. Hmmm. Why would she say "unless?" Surely she still planned to marry him once he proved he could change.

In no mood for confrontation when he had been seeking a pleasant evening, he decided not to call her on her slip of the tongue. Perhaps that's all it was—an innocent slip of the tongue from a nervous prospective bride.

"I hope your situation is not too dire." Cecil tilted his head toward what was left of the fire. "You certainly seem to be economizing on wood."

"I am not," she protested. "I had retired for the night and had not planned to be in this room again until tomorrow afternoon. Your unexpected arrival necessitated my having to dress again."

"So sorry to have bothered you."

"Why did you come here without notice?"

"You are such a poor correspondent, I was hoping you might like to see my progress for yourself."

"I can see it." He'd heard more emotion in her voice when she was placing an order with Gunther's. Olivia leaned over and sniffed the air around him. "The stench of tobacco about your person—it is gone." She leaned back in her chair and crossed her arms. "Have you indeed quit, or is it just for this evening to try to make me believe you are making progress?"

"Did I take a glass of port here tonight? Or brandy? Or a mug of ale?"

"Did you?"

He chortled. Hearing himself, he realized he didn't like the bitter edge his laughter held. "What did the maid report to you? I notice you instructed her to tempt me not only once but three times."

"I did not," she protested too quickly.

Cecil rubbed his chin. "I have known you long enough to tell when you are lying, Olivia. Did you really think I would accept the offer here in your very house if I wanted to convince you of my sincerity?"

"If you had accepted her offer, I had planned not to see you." She lifted her nose in his direction.

"Is that the truth? You can discard me as firmly as all that without so much as a farewell?"

Olivia's features slackened with obvious guilt. "Of course not. I–I just wanted to see how well you are doing. And I see that you are coming along splendidly."

"Thank you." Even though Cecil had already eaten, he harbored hope that she might offer him a bite to eat while they chatted over things inconsequential, even if it meant warmed-over mutton from the night's dinner. Still she made no move to display any hospitality. Not even an offer for a second cup of tea.

"How the night passes quickly," she said.

"Too quickly." He looked at the grandfather clock with a motion broad enough to attract her notice. "I suppose I shall be going." He did not rise, hoping she would deter him.

"I wish you could stay," she said with no emotion, "but I have an early day tomorrow."

"You plan to rise before noon, my dear?"

She bristled. "I have an important meeting."

He waited for her to elaborate, but she didn't. He rose from his seat since he could no longer delay the inevitable.

"I am pleased with your progress. I wish you a good evening and anticipate our meeting again when the year is up."

"But my dear, I do believe that I shall be ready before then."

"But our agreement was for a year." Olivia's voice exuded a strange tone, almost as though she didn't want him to succeed, and certainly no sooner than in the space of a year.

"In any event," she continued, "I have no idea whether or not your manners have improved."

"I assure you, they have. I am taking lessons. If you would spend an evening with me, you would see for yourself."

"I would find that agreeable, no doubt," she said, "but I am afraid I have my social calendar quite full for the time being."

"If you say so, my dear. No doubt you are much sought after. Might you offer me any details?"

She looked at the floor, though she didn't bow her head in shame. "I hold a box at the opera, as you know, and I have received quite a few invitations for festivities here in town." Apparently satisfied that she had given him a reasonable explanation, she returned her gaze to his face. "What a shame you are out there all alone in the dreary country with no one to entertain you but the wild beasts and other rustic types."

"And what a shame you are forced to attend the opera and festivities alone." He knew better but decided not to embarrass her further by waiting for an excuse, one that would no doubt be a lie. "Good night, Olivia. Do not bother to show me to the door."

Cecil donned his hat and coat to depart into a brisk night. He wasn't certain which was colder—Olivia or the evening air. He had felt more warmth over business with his solicitor. Since his proposal of marriage, Olivia had changed. Instead of making him feel like a man in love, she treated him like a mother giving approval to a little boy. During the course of their interview, Cecil discovered he didn't need the protection, admonition, and judgment of a mother enough to relish the feeling.

He entered the cab and almost told the driver to take the coach to Lizzie's if for no other reason than to spite Olivia. But he was in no mood for female companionship of any sort. He instructed the coachman to deliver him to his home.

As they passed street after street, he realized that Olivia had not even bothered to inquire about her cousin, Eunice.

Once he was home and prepared to retire for the evening, bittersweet emotions roiled through him. Seeing Olivia hadn't had the effect on him that he anticipated. And if her frigid attitude toward him was an indication, his visit was evoking no emotion in her. How odd for a woman who was considering becoming engaged to him! He contemplated the past few years. He had thought himself in love and fancied that she returned his feelings. How could he have been so mistaken?

Not that he was lovable. He knew he had his faults. He had thought for a time that Olivia's tolerance of his adventures was her way of expressing her love. Perhaps it was her way of showing her indifference.

No doubt Olivia had made good on her threat to seek other suitors. She was still an attractive woman and, more importantly to men of modest means, an unwed woman with a reasonable, though not extravagant, income and no troublesome relatives to stake a claim to her fortune. At least, no relatives had made themselves known. To men of means, Olivia had proven herself a popular hostess and was still of childbearing age. Both of these factors enhanced her ability to attract other men. Men who, perhaps, were less adventurous, who seemed more docile and willing to be manipulated to Olivia's every whim.

But if Cecil himself was not docile, who was? He had already agreed to change his mode of living to suit her. He shuddered in self-disgust.

"Bah! What was I thinking? I could be enjoying a glass of

port and a fine cigar and a good meal, as well." He patted his belly and noticed, not for the first time, that it had decreased in size since he had modified his diet. He wished he didn't have to admit it, but he felt better, too. Olivia or no Olivia, those benefits were the real reasons he shouldn't let himself backslide.

And then there was Eunice. Even though she was assigned only to teach him manners, she was willing to accept him with or without a polished facade. She was only changing him for Olivia's sake, not because she herself had asked him to change. He supposed he owed Abigail no small amount of thanks. Although she was too courteous to make broad mention of it, he was aware that she had asked Eunice to assist him. If not for Abigail, he was sure that Eunice would never have considered helping him. And why should she have, after the way he had tried to kiss her in the garden?

Though the sting of pain was long past, Cecil rubbed his right cheek in remembrance. As much as he wished Eunice had given in to the kiss, he respected her much more for her rebuff.

Except for Abigail, Eunice was the first woman he had come into regular contact with who took her Bible seriously. No doubt her love of scripture and its admonitions spurred Eunice to remain chaste in every way. No wonder she wanted him to read the Bible as well. He speculated that the words would offer him something he had been missing for a long time. Perhaps she was right.

Instead of going straight to bed as he had planned, Cecil kept the candle on his nightstand burning, sat in a chair, and opened his Bible. Over time, he had grown to love the four Gospels most. Jesus seemed so gentle, yet Cecil could imagine His voice becoming stern when He was admonishing the sinners of His time to improve the way they treated their neighbors—and themselves.

Swallowing, Cecil could also well imagine that Jesus would chastise him first and foremost if He were to return that day. Cecil avoided the book of Revelation with the fervor that those living in Bible times avoided lepers. He knew he was still a babe in Christ, so much so that the prophetic passages left him in fear and trembling. But why?

Just as quickly as the question occurred to him, he could answer it.

God wanted more from him. He knew it. Eunice showed him how the Lord wanted His own to live, and Cecil understood that though he would never be perfect, he could aspire to a better life—a life of more significance—than the one he had been leading all these years. If he had lived as he should have all along, he never would have lost Abigail. And Olivia might love him instead of treating him like yesterday's rubbish.

God's commands were meant not only to please Himself but to make life better for the people He created. Cecil could see that now.

❧

"Lord Giles and Lady Violet have come to call, milady," the butler told Eunice.

Eunice and her aunt were known to be at home on Thursday afternoons, so the fact they had callers was no surprise. The callers' identities were another matter, since neither woman was well acquainted with either guest.

"Lord Giles and Lady Violet! Oh, my, how exciting! Send them in," Aunt May instructed. "And bring tea and biscuits immediately."

"Yes, milady." He gave them a quick bow and departed.

"But Auntie, they will not be expecting refreshments for a short visit," Eunice protested, making sure to keep her voice gentle. Aunt May was already in the process of compiling her invitation list for social occasions, and to her mind, Lord Giles and Lady Violet would be esteemed guests to add.

"A little good food never hurt either body or soul." Aunt May looked out the window. Eunice followed her lead and noted a dark and dreary sky. "Especially when they have come all this way on such a miserable day."

Unable to argue the point, Eunice followed Aunt May to the parlor where they always received callers. They had concentrated their first labors on that room in particular, and their efforts showed. Botanical wallpaper with delicate pink roses on a cream-colored background looked fresh. Eunice and her aunt had agreed upon new velvet draperies in a deep green to compliment the flower stems on the paper. Eunice had been pleased with the result. The rich fabric added elegance to their surroundings and picked up the deep green stripes in both the sofa and the winged chairs. The finest pieces of mahogany furniture in the house—a rocking chair, tea table, and two other occasional tables—found their place here. Polished to a sheen, the select pieces fashioned of coveted wood discreetly told their visitors that the home was occupied by fine ladies.

If doubt remained, guests needed only to look upon the two full-length portraits of Grandmamma and Grandpapa. The oil paintings were larger than life, together occupying the entire west wall. Grandmamma was in her prime, a new bride lounging in the formal gardens, dressed in the best finery of her day. She held in the crook of her arm a spoiled-looking dog with long white hair. Grandpapa, apparently in another part of the gardens, likewise cut a fine figure in his military uniform that was decorated with ribbons and pins bestowed by the king's army for bravery in battle. Two well-groomed hunting dogs stood by his side.

These were not the portraits painted by traveling artists—the ones who painted dresses and suits ahead of time and filled in a subject's head once the portrait was commissioned. No. The artist must have spent months depicting them in the finery they once owned. Eunice had the clothing in the attic wardrobe to prove it. Of every item in the room, Eunice was most proud of her portraits. One could purchase furniture, rugs, and statues. Family could not be bought at any price.

Eunice allowed herself a contented sigh as she straightened the lines of her dress so that the fabric sat in a neat line against the sofa. A welcoming fire crackled, emitting the pleasant scent of burning pine into the room. Perhaps the rest of the house left something to be desired, but surely the parlor had become a masterpiece of exquisite taste.

Sir Giles entered with the flourish expected according to his reputation, as though the occupants of the room had been waiting for him with rapt anticipation and the advent of his arrival meant that life could begin at the manor house. Lady Violet followed closely behind him, looking afraid of her shadow as she always did when she was a little girl. Had Lady Violet not been announced, Eunice wouldn't have recognized her. They had made brief acquaintance when they were both girls. Violet had become plump, and her hair had darkened over the years. Eunice swept her hands over her dress in a move of sudden self-consciousness. Had she changed so in the past decade?

As the four of them chatted, Eunice was pleased to discover that Violet might be a kindred spirit. Her brother, in the meantime, flirted with her aunt in the overly gallant way that a handsome young man might employ to flatter an elderly lady who wouldn't misconstrue his attentions as sincere. The looks and subtle observations he sent Eunice's way were not the flowery speech of Lord Milton but seemed to convey a serious undertone. Eunice squirmed. Surely any woman would be pleased to draw Lord Giles's attention, but she chose to withhold her judgment. A man's relationship with the Lord weighed far more heavily with Eunice than his title, appearance, or fortune.

"Miss Norwood," Lord Giles said, interrupting her musings, "I understand you have been teaching Lord Sutton his manners."

Taken aback, Eunice felt herself blush. Had she and Cecil become the subject of local gossip? For Cecil's sake, she wanted to deny she was giving him lessons at all, but her faith and personal integrity stopped her. "I—I did not realize that the lessons were common knowledge."

"So the rumors are true."

"Lord Giles, if the purpose of your visit is to gossip—"

"No, of course not," Violet intervened. "I am delighted to talk about the weather, if it means we can enjoy your hospitality."

Eunice sent Violet a grateful smile.

"Of course, I agree with my sister wholeheartedly," Sir Giles said. "But any rumor circulating about the lessons would only serve to compliment you, Miss Norwood. I am sure that anyone who notices an improvement in Cecil would have to attribute such a development to something—or someone." His eyes twinkled. "So tell me, if I were to spill my cup of tea now, would you give me lessons as well?"

Aunt May laughed too loudly and added, "Such a drastic action is hardly necessary."

"And I seriously doubt you need any lessons," Eunice said.

"And Giles," Violet said, "I seriously doubt that Miss Norwood harbors a secret desire to run an etiquette school for wayward lords."

Lord Giles laughed. "I suppose not. But really, Miss Norwood, do you think anyone can help someone as hopeless as Cecil?"

"He is not hopeless."

"Oh?" Giles took an exaggerated swallow of tea.

"No one is," Eunice replied.

"So you say. But if you will allow me to say so, I believe your time would be much better spent in more refined company."

Eunice could see that Sir Giles referred to himself. Did he mean to hint that he hoped to see more of her? She decided to try diplomacy mixed with a touch of humor. "I believe I am doing as you suggest at this very moment, Lord Giles."

"And we would be delighted to see more of you," Aunt May hastened to add, "along with you, Lady Violet, of course."

"Of course." Lady Violet rose from her seat, and her brother rose as well. "Regrettably, we must be leaving. Our visit with you, Lady May and Miss Norwood, has been our pleasure."

"I could not agree more." Lord Giles extended his hand and brushed his lips against her aunt's wrist for an instant. He then bowed and placed his lips on Eunice's wrist, lingering a touch longer than necessary for an old friend. The gesture reminded her of the embellished manners of Lord Milton. For no apparent reason, she felt uncomfortable enough to withdraw her hand as quickly as etiquette allowed without portraying rudeness. As they departed, Lord Giles looked back at her once more, then, obviously embarrassed at being caught, turned away just as quickly when their eyes met.

Funny, meeting Lord Giles's gaze didn't give her the same sweet tingle that she felt whenever she swam in the blue of Cecil's eyes.

The brother and sister hadn't been gone but a moment when Aunt May nearly jumped up and down, clapping with joy. "I do believe we can invite them to our dinner. How delightful!" She nudged Eunice. "Lord Giles has taken a liking to you, you know."

"Don't be silly, Auntie." Nevertheless, she felt heat rise to her face.

"Silly, indeed. I may be old, but I remember being a young woman. He intends to ask my permission to court you. I can see it in his face."

"Oh, really, Auntie. He was just putting on an agreeable expression since theirs was a social call."

"Of course he was. But I could read the light in his eyes and the attention he paid to you. Each time you spoke, he couldn't stop looking at you or listening with more intent than most men would pay to their solicitors."

Eunice chuckled. "I hope I do possess more appeal than a solicitor."

"Indeed you do, and the local gentlemen are starting to notice." Aunt May let out a sigh and looked about the room. "Before I know it, you'll be marrying and moving to another estate. I shall spend the rest of my days alone here in this old house."

"Oh, I would never let you live alone, Auntie. I love you too much."

Aunt May's eyes misted. She took Eunice's young hand in her wrinkled one and squeezed it. "Lord Giles has much to offer—a good family name, land holdings, wealth. . . ."

"I know. But I already have those things."

"Yes, which means that such a match would increase your influence and assure your future progeny a bright future. How could any woman not notice he is handsome? And," Aunt May pointed out, "unencumbered."

Eunice didn't have to ask Aunt May to elaborate. Clearly she referred to Cecil and his plans to become engaged to Olivia once the year had passed. Were her feelings for Cecil so transparent? She felt blood rise to her cheeks at the thought.

"Lord Giles would make you happy. I'm sure of it. He would be an excellent match for you. An excellent match, indeed."

seven

The following Sunday, the servants didn't awaken Cecil early. They had no reason to bother. Worn out on Saturday evening from a day of hunting with Tedric, by the time he retired, he had yet to decide if he would attend worship services the following day. He decided not to leave instructions to awaken him at all.

So when he awoke on his own early enough to attend, a mixture of surprise, happiness, and dread filled his being. He realized that fear played a part, too. Cecil hadn't set foot in any church—either in the country or in London—in more than a decade. Though he would rather be struck by lightning than admit his feelings to anyone, the thought of returning to church sent his stomach into a frenzy of somersaults.

Remaining in bed, he picked up the silver bell on the nightstand and rang it to summon Luke.

His faithful valet responded quickly to the bell. Cecil was a bit taken aback to see Luke dressed in a suit as fine as any servant could expect to afford. He sat up in bed. "Where are you going, Luke?"

Luke looked at Cecil as though he had taken leave of his senses. "Why, to church, milord."

He hesitated. "Yes. But of course."

What was he thinking? Naturally, the servants attended church services. Tedric would never deny his staff the privilege. Cecil supposed his servants in London worshiped on Sunday mornings as well. How would he know one way or the other? Exhausted from the previous evening's festivities, he often slept until the noon hour on the Sabbath.

He lifted his voice with pride. "So am I."

"You are what, milord?"

"I will be attending church this morning." To prove he was serious, he rose.

Luke gasped. "You are, milord?"

"Yes. Is that really such a surprise?"

"If I may be permitted to say so, milord. But a happy one, indeed."

Cecil chuckled. "You are permitted. Now then, I need you to help me find my prayer book." Cecil didn't want to confess that he hadn't bothered to keep track of the book he would need to participate in worship services. He hadn't looked at it since he became a confirmed member of the Church of England as a young adult, a commitment expected of him by his community, his family, and God.

"I think your prayer book may be in the library, milord."

"A very good deduction," Cecil said. "Fetch me the book and my suit and have breakfast brought up."

"Yes, milord. If I may say so, we will have to hurry if we hope to arrive at the church before the service begins."

"Noted. But a man must eat."

"Indeed, milord." He bowed and hurried to complete his errands.

Later, Cecil enjoyed the hearty breakfast of sausage and eggs brought up to his room, but then hurried out in hopes of catching up with Tedric's carriage. Unsuccessful, he followed them on his own horse. He couldn't remember the last time he had risen so early on Sunday. As he rode along, the day seemed somehow more peaceful than all the rest.

Soon he entered the sanctuary. The Savior's house appeared smaller than he remembered. When he had served as an altar boy all those years ago, the aisle seemed long as he carried the cross. The altar, fashioned of carved dark wood, was much as he remembered. The stained-glass windows were the same. He presumed the sturdy, colorful pictures of brave and worthy Christians and of Christ Himself would survive long after his own death. He clutched the prayer book more tightly and searched for the Sutton family pew, the front one on the left.

He was just about to approach the pew when he heard gasps and whispers. To his horror, everyone in church had turned to stare at him. Some turned away when he returned their stares. Others muttered comments to their fellow worshipers. Mouths dropped open and eyes widened. Did everyone feel the need to react to his return?

He set his gaze on his brother and sister-in-law. Cecil could see from their tight lips and eyes that Tedric and Abigail were doing everything within their power not to express their shock and delight. Tedric sent him a short nod to indicate that he was welcome to sit by them. But since the Sutton family pew was located in the front near the pulpit, Cecil thought better than to join them. He was already the topic of gossip; there was no need to fuel the fire by sitting in such a prominent place.

Eager to get away from the congregation's curious wonderment, he looked for Eunice. He spotted her and her aunt occupying a pew near the back of the sanctuary. Eunice's expression looked friendly and open and conveyed considerably less surprise than anyone else's. No wonder. Eunice was now the person who knew him best—even better than his own family.

He took a few steps toward them, then stopped short. Sharing private lessons in etiquette was one matter, but one's public appearance was quite another. Would a lady as devout as Eunice spurn him in front of everyone in church? Would she forbid him, a cad, to sit beside her in the Savior's house? The kind look on her face didn't diminish one iota, but he still wasn't sure. Nevertheless, he drew up the courage to walk over toward her pew.

He bent toward her so that he could be heard by Eunice alone. "Good morning, Miss Norwood. May I have the honor of sharing your pew?"

"But of course." Her lack of hesitation surprised and pleased him.

"Thank you for your indulgence." He took his seat on the end of the row, then nodded toward her aunt and Brigadier General Tarkington, who sat beside Eunice. Unlike Eunice, they dropped their mouths in shock. Aunt May's eyes seemed to hold a sympathetic cast, but the brigadier general sniffed and turned his head toward the pulpit.

Cecil didn't flinch. No matter what the military man thought of him, he refused to acknowledge the snub. He cut a sideways glance toward Eunice and saw that her eyes lit with pleasure. Her opinion was what mattered. He withheld a satisfied smile.

His moment in pleasure was short-lived. Whispers fluttered throughout the church. Surely people were speculating about his unexpected presence at worship, Eunice's willingness to allow him to sit beside her, or both. Cecil refused to stare at those whose heads snapped in his direction, then quickly turned away. He averted his eyes to his shoes, as though studying them would amend his guilt.

He was almost relieved when he felt a tap on his shoulder. The distraction was welcome. A friend who had summoned the courage to greet him with warmth, perhaps? He looked up and faced Giles.

"Do you mind moving over a bit, Cecil?" Giles's expression was a mixture of cockiness and curiosity.

Seeing that Giles didn't want to greet him but rather to move in on his territory, Cecil tried not to look grumpy. "I would not mind in the least, except that, as you can plainly see, this pew is becoming crowded."

"There is always room for one more." Giles stepped forward, forcing Cecil to move lest he be sat upon. At least Cecil managed to hold on to his place beside Eunice, though he suspected this development disappointed Giles. Cecil cut his gaze to Eunice's aunt and the brigadier general. They greeted Giles cordially, but he took pleasure in noting that Eunice was more reserved. Eunice sent Cecil a shy but approving look, a fact that pleased him even more.

Cecil kept himself anchored to the pew, his girth separating Eunice from Giles. Although worship services were hardly a conducive place to conduct a conversation of any sort, clearly Giles's intent was to position himself—literally—where he could enjoy Eunice's nearness. Cecil remembered the sly comments Giles had made about Eunice when he first discovered that she had returned to the country. He should have known then that Giles looked at Eunice with more than friendship on his mind.

And why shouldn't he? Giles cut a dashing figure—more dashing than Cecil, though he would never admit the unfavorable comparison to anyone but himself. A man whose modest inheritance allowed him a comfortable living, Giles could give a woman a good name. Why shouldn't he believe himself suitable for Eunice?

And Eunice herself! She would make any man an extraordinary wife. Her blond beauty meant that she didn't need a fortune to attract suitors. Yet her uncle Eric's fortune, house, and land holdings most likely surpassed the assets of at least half the genteel families in the parish.

Eric had been known for shrewd business practices. His lands were rented out for use by local farmers, who paid handsome rents. He had undertaken a keen study of animal husbandry and agriculture. His efforts paid off with abundant crops and hearty livestock. During more than one lean year, Eric was able to coax the land to yield a crop when others nearby failed. Yet the late earl also enjoyed a reputation of a kind man, one who was never cruel, dishonest, or merciless. Eric was the first to feed the needy, send local widows generous Christmas food baskets, and help neighbors in times of trouble. From all accounts, his reputation was well deserved.

All of these facts Cecil knew simply from his years as a semiresident of Sutton Manor. Yet since Eunice's arrival, he had learned more. Cecil and Eunice had shared more than lessons; they had shared tea and conversation. Eunice confessed that even though Eric was a skilled businessman, he had proven inept in managing the life of his young niece, a girl thrust upon him by default after the death of his youngest sister, since May was busy tending to their sick mother at the time. Wanting to be a good uncle but helpless when faced with a dependent girl, Eric sent her off to a reputable though indifferent boarding school and hoped for the best.

Eunice had confided to Cecil that her time there was not among her fondest memories. When she requested a pound or two for clothing, Eric favored practical and inexpensive cotton and wool the servants spun on his estate to the imported silks a young woman of Eunice's station was expected to wear on grand occasions. He considered ribbons and other embellishments a waste. Eunice always felt out of place among the other girls and was more content to spend time in the library or with her sewing. The result was that many of her classmates mistook Eunice for a near-poverty case or for an eccentric rather than for the refined lady she was.

As Eunice had confided the reality of her past, Cecil found himself admiring the fact that her voice held no bitterness or rancor. He had long ago concluded that no yardage of ribbons nor any number of exquisite buttons or other trims could have transformed his serious and studious Eunice into a frivolous coquette. He smiled at an image he formed in his mind, a fantasy of Eunice gaining high marks while her foolish classmates barely passed their courses.

He glanced at Giles. How could such a dandy hope to keep a thoughtful woman such as Eunice happy? Although Giles did not bear the black marks on his reputation that Cecil had earned, he was still nothing more than a vapid peacock. Yet for all his flaws, Giles was far more suitable for Eunice than Cecil, a cad who was learning manners to woo her cousin.

Olivia. A picture of her formed in his mind. She was scolding him, ridiculing him, telling him both directly and indirectly that she disdained him. An even more undesirable picture of Olivia dancing with that dog Loughton popped into his head. He shook it out and tried to concentrate on the order of worship.

ça

As Eunice read through the order of worship along with the rest of the congregation, she eyed Cecil sitting beside her and Giles beyond. If she harbored any doubts about Lord Giles's intentions, his insistence on sitting on her pew—even going so far as to push Cecil over—left no doubt that Lord Giles would soon be asking her aunt if he would be allowed to court her. Yet instead of desiring the attentions of an eligible bachelor, she longed for one who was no longer eligible.

Cecil. Happiness filled her heart when he asked to sit with her. Why did the gossips have to deny her what small amount of pleasure she could derive from being near him? Not one to call attention to herself, Eunice squirmed when suddenly her pew had become the source of entertainment. Why, she wondered, did they seem to condemn a man who was making a valiant effort to reenter the life of the church?

They should be rejoicing at his return.

With a deliberate motion, she tilted her nose slightly skyward. She, for one, was glad Cecil had come to worship. She was entitled to sit beside anyone she wished during church. Wagging tongues would never cause her to hold her head down in shame.

Eunice recognized a few of the faces that turned to stare at them however briefly. Why did they insist on commenting on matters that were none of their concern? Perhaps they thought Cecil was interfering with the friendship between her and Giles. She suspected that many in the parish overestimated the significance of her acquaintance with Giles. No doubt Aunt May played a role in their misinterpretation. Her aunt considered Lord Giles a good match for Eunice, in spite of her protests that Giles held no fascination for her. Yet Aunt May would not be opposed to everyone in the village assuming that he was about to embark on a courtship with her niece.

Whatever their reasons, she could tell from their snobbish expressions that their thoughts were not pleasant. Eunice watched one of the women send a mean look Cecil's way. Maybe she was mistaken. Maybe they weren't thinking of Eunice and Giles but only of Cecil. She was all too aware that Cecil hadn't set foot in church in years. He had admitted the fact himself.

They may live near Cecil now, but he is a stranger to them. They have not witnessed our lessons or Cecil's willingness to read the Bible. They have no notion as to how much he has changed.

Despite her reassurances to herself, Eunice felt her cheeks burn. Throughout the service, she held her head up and looked the vicar straight in the eye as he preached.

"Thou shalt love thy neighbour as thyself." The words of Christ rang in her ear, seemingly sent to her as a message from heaven during the benediction. Shutting the hymnal, she

caught a glimpse of two matrons eyeing them, then giggling like young girls. Eunice wished she could stroll up to them and suggest they read Matthew 19:19. If not for her reluctance to embarrass her aunt, she might well have given in to her impulse.

Cecil nodded a farewell to her and hurried out of the church. Not that she blamed him. If she had been subjected to as many stares and whispers as he, especially in the Lord's house, Eunice would have fled after the benediction, too. Watching him leave, she wished she could invite him to Sunday dinner. A firm shake of her aunt's head told her not to dare. Just as quickly, she nodded once toward Giles, indicating she might invite him to dinner. Eunice decided not to respond to the silent hint.

Thankfully, the brigadier general shared an anecdote with them on the way out of the sanctuary. For a time, Aunt May tittered with amusement at his story, and Eunice sent a polite nod now and again. Her aunt's chatter gave Eunice a feeling that perhaps she wasn't upset.

The sense of security was false, a fact she discovered as soon as the door of the carriage shut behind them. Aunt May set her mouth in an unwavering line and huffed. Since her aunt was sitting directly across from Eunice, she could experience the full impact of Aunt May's displeasure. She began with a disapproving shake of her head.

Eunice swallowed. "Vicar Mooring gave an excellent sermon today, did he not?"

"Vicar Mooring always gives an excellent sermon. Not that I could listen to it while experiencing a fit of apoplexy."

"Apoplexy?"

"Yes. Apoplexy." Aunt May huffed. "The thought of having to share my pew with such a. . .such a—a. . ."

"Christian?"

Aunt May's eyes narrowed. "Do not make light of what I have to say. You know perfectly well that was not what I was thinking. I want to know why you allowed that awful man to sit beside you in church today." Her voice was so shrill that Eunice barely recognized it as belonging to her beloved aunt.

Eunice wasn't sure how to answer. "What awful man?"

"Lord Sutton, of course," Aunt May responded in a studiously even voice, indicating her patience with Eunice was evaporating.

A pang of hurt shot through Eunice. How could Aunt May berate Cecil? She hardly knew him. Despite her fear of incurring her aunt's wrath, Eunice had to defend him. "But Auntie, you allow me to go to Sutton Manor and teach him etiquette on a regular basis. How could I spurn him in church and call myself a Christian?"

"As your guardian, my task is not to answer philosophical questions but to see to it that you conduct yourself in a manner befitting your birth. Your mention of the lessons brings me to another point, one I have been meaning to express for some time." She leaned closer to Eunice. "I know I encouraged you to teach him as a favor to your dear friend. And I think your visits to Sutton Manor have resulted in a quite pleasant renewal of your acquaintance with Abigail."

Eunice thought about the happy times she had shared with her friend since returning to the country. "I agree most heartily."

"But I must ask how much etiquette exists in the world for you to teach anyone, even someone as reprehensible as Lord Sutton. Surely the lessons should be coming to a close soon."

"And they shall. But now we are undertaking a study of great literature. I told him that all gentlemen should be educated."

"And has he not been educated?"

"Certainly so. But he has not darkened the door of the

library in years. A rereading of the classics is in order, I think. And you will be so pleased to know that we are including the Bible in his studies."

"Of course that pleases me, but you are not the vicar."

"No, but the vicar has many parishioners, while I have none. Surely we need to discuss Cecil's progress and what he has read."

Aunt May sniffed. "Such subjects are far more suited to be approached by the mind of a man than by that of a woman. If Lord Sutton has anything to discuss, he can approach his brother." Obviously satisfied that she had made her point, she sat back in her seat.

"But Abigail—"

"You can still visit Abigail without the flimsy pretext of teaching manners to her brother-in-law. In fact, I encourage it."

Eunice hugged her Bible to her chest. At least her aunt wasn't forbidding Eunice to go to the Sutton estate. Surely she would be able to see Cecil.

"I see that smile on your face," Aunt May noted. "Do not think I approve of Lord Sutton. I never did. I never have. And I never will."

Eunice felt her eyes widen. She couldn't remember her aunt ever being so harsh. "But Auntie, he has come so far—"

"Not far enough to continue his association with you, I'm afraid. The way everyone reacted to his presence in church today should be proof enough."

Eunice felt her face flush hot when she remembered the murmurs that reverberated throughout the church when Cecil sat beside her.

"If you allow him to appear as more than an acquaintance toward you in such a public place, no doubt your reputation will soon be damaged beyond repair."

"I do not judge a person by what others think. Our Lord and

Savior cautioned us not to judge, lest we should be judged."

" 'And with what measure ye mete, it shall be measured to you again.' " Aunt May crossed her arms. "Since I do not live the life of a reprobate and because the death of my brother has left you within the realm of my responsibility, I believe it is my duty to render judgment where appropriate. And I judge Lord Sutton to be unfit for your company except on those occasions when you are teaching him to help your friend. So with that judgment in mind, I forbid you to see Lord Sutton again."

eight

Eunice didn't bother to hold back a gasp. How could her aunt, usually so loving and kind, deliver such a harsh edict? "Never see him again?"

"That is what I said."

The carriage pulled to a stop in front of the manor house.

"I suggest we not discuss this any further." Aunt May disembarked before Eunice could object.

Perhaps Aunt May was right. Eunice needed to absorb the impact of this unexpected edict. In the course of a few days, Eunice had journeyed from feeling victorious in her efforts to help Cecil to being banished from his presence. Her throat tightened at the thought. Unable to speak, she hurried her pace so it was just short of a run. She rushed up the steps, through the front door, and scurried over the curved stairs to her room. She had to refresh her toilette for Sunday dinner. Eunice looked straight ahead and made sure to avoid eye contact with anyone. She didn't want the servants to see her cry.

As they sat down to dinner an hour later and Aunt May said grace, Eunice could barely concentrate on the lovely roast of beef, gravy, parsnips, and potatoes set before her. Under any other circumstances, she would have found delight in such a savory offering. But upset by the prospect of not seeing Cecil again, she found her appetite lacking.

Aunt May, pretending that nothing was amiss, talked about the sermon as she usually did, asking Eunice's opinion from time to time. Eunice was too upset to do much more than agree with her aunt's observations.

"Eunice," Aunt May finally said after she had reviewed every sentence of the message, "must you pick at your dinner?"

"Everything is very good, but I am not hungry, Aunt May."

"Really! Are you so besotted with that terrible man?" Aunt May patted her mouth with her napkin with more flourish than needed.

"I am not besotted. And please do not keep referring to Cecil in such unflattering terms."

"Your defense of him only proves that you are indeed besotted."

Unwilling to argue with her aunt, Eunice took a sip of tea.

"You cannot deny it. I thought so. But my dear, your feelings are pointless," Aunt May observed. "Do you not remember that he is thinking of a betrothal to your cousin Olivia? What kind of family relation would you be to try to steal her fiancé away from her?"

"Olivia does not love him."

Aunt May laughed. "Silly goose. They have been courting for years. Of course she does."

"She does not. She told me so herself."

"I do not believe it. Why would she share such a confidence with you, a cousin she barely knows?"

"I am not sure she set out to share her feelings with me, but she mentioned it in conversation. I really have no notion that she even wants to marry at all."

"How absurd," Aunt May said between bites of food. "Every woman wants to wed."

"But you did not."

"No." Aunt May's eyes grew sad, and her features slackened with regret. "My beau was shot in the colonies' revolt. I had no offers after that."

"I am sorry. I know you would have made a fine wife."

"That is in the past. Too long ago to even think of anymore."

Aunt May reached over and patted her hand. "I am concerned now with your welfare and with the peace of this family."

"I know, and I love you for it, Aunt May. But I have done nothing wrong, nor do I intend to." Eunice took a sip of tea and let the reassuring warm liquid comfort her body and soul.

"Then you must remember, whether or not Olivia loves him, or if he loves her, is none of your affair," Aunt May said. "You were asked to help your cousin, not to hinder her marriage. And while love is a nice thing, it is a luxury. Most of the women I know marry to increase their fortunes."

"If she is marrying for money, then that hardly makes Olivia honorable. If she were a better stewardess of the money she has, she would not need to marry a man she does not love just to increase her fortune."

"Her honor is her own affair and between God and herself. Her intentions are not for you to judge."

"I can assess the situation when it affects me and act accordingly," Eunice assured her.

"My, what a worldly attitude. I do believe his bad characteristics are affecting you for the worse, Eunice. All the more reason why you should not see him anymore."

"But I have no notion that I can avoid seeing him. You already said I am free to visit Abigail."

"True. Though I wish she were not related to such a sorry brother-in-law, I do not think your friendship should be compromised."

"But Cecil is trying to change," Eunice said. "In fact, he has changed."

"Then how did he summon up the nerve to go to church after all these years and ask to sit with us in our family pew? Why did his own brother not allow him to sit with his family?"

"Tedric and Abigail would not have turned him away. They would never do such a thing, no matter how badly he might have behaved in the past."

"Then why did he ask to sit with us?"

Eunice thought for a moment. "I do not know. Perhaps he arrived at our pew first."

"Yes, we are closer to the back. How convenient."

"How unfortunate. His action made the situation so much more difficult for the local gossips, who had to turn their heads to see him." Eunice knew her voice held the edge of the sarcasm she couldn't help but convey.

"They turned their heads and whispered in disbelief, no doubt. How dare he return to our church after all these years." Aunt May's voice took on a hard edge that Eunice wasn't accustomed to hearing from her.

"Aunt May, I beg your pardon, but I am quite shocked that you would object. You are well aware I am teaching him manners. To deny him a seat in our pew would have been the height of rudeness. How could I not act like a lady when I am teaching him how to be a gentleman? Can you deny that the very fact he is going to church is a sign that he is making progress?

"A point that only proves that he no longer needs lessons."

"You did not seem to object when Lord Giles asked to sit with us," Eunice couldn't help but point out. "After he forced us to squeeze together so, I wondered how any of us could breathe at all. Certainly he could have sat with his sister, Lady Violet."

"Of course. But I do believe I saw Lady Violet with Sir Roderick."

"Oh, they are courting?"

"Yes, and I believe there will be a marriage proposal from Sir Roderick soon. Really, Eunice, how could you not have known? You really do need to get out more." Aunt May stirred her tea. "And that is yet another good reason why you no longer need to see Lord Sutton. He is consuming far too much of your time, when you could be looking over potential marriage prospects here. And I do believe Brigadier General Tarkington would more than agree."

The mention of Brigadier General Tarkington caused Eunice to see her aunt's real motive. The local gossips didn't bother her any more than they did Eunice. But Aunt May did care what her new suitor thought. Eunice sensed that the stern and disciplined military man would have no patience with an idle gentleman such as Cecil.

She decided not to argue—at least for the time being. She rose from her seat and hugged her aunt. "Oh, Auntie dear, let us not quarrel. By your leave, I would like to be excused so that I might work on my embroidery. Perhaps you might enjoy sitting by the fire with me and reading a good book."

"I would enjoy reading, but I do believe I prefer a nap instead, thank you," Aunt May said. "But you may not be excused quite yet. Before you indulge yourself in your needlework, you have a letter to write."

Eunice searched her mind. She couldn't remember any unanswered correspondence.

"I want you to write Lord Sutton a letter to inform him that your lessons together are being discontinued immediately."

"A letter? But should I not tell him in person?" she asked. "I think that would be far more polite. In any event, I have promised Abigail I will soon visit her. She has just completed a new tapestry. I certainly want to admire her handiwork."

Aunt May sighed. For a moment, Eunice wondered if she planned to allow the sigh to serve as her answer. The two women sat in silence. Eunice listened to the fire crackle and watched her aunt breathe more deeply than usual, as was her habit when she was deep in contemplation.

She finally answered. "All right, then. You may go to the

estate and tell him in person. But I warn you, giving in to your wish is against my better judgment."

"Thank you, Aunt May."

Eunice didn't remember a time when she was more grateful to have a wish granted.

Later, alone with her needlework, Eunice recalled the morning's events—including the quarrel with her aunt. The remembrance of such unpleasantness played a sour note in her mind. She never wanted to displease her beloved aunt. Yet despite her aunt's upset, Eunice knew she had to defend herself—and Cecil.

The idea that she had to tell Cecil about the lessons' discontinuance in person wasn't totally true. Though she knew that delivering the bad news in person might take away some of its sting, a letter would have sufficed. Guilt reared its ugly head. In her heart, Eunice knew that for some time she had been using the lessons as a way to keep seeing Cecil. She wasn't sure whether Cecil noticed or not, but if he did, he never indicated that he minded in the least. If anything, he seemed even happier to see her with each passing lesson.

Though she was not a worldly woman, Eunice could see by the way he let his look linger upon her, how he studied her face when he thought she wasn't looking, how he let his hand linger too long on hers, and by the sweet words that flowed from his lips that his interest in her was sincere. If it weren't, would he have agreed to read a challenging author such as Shakespeare? Would he have cracked open his dusty Bible?

Would he have attended church?

She didn't think so. At that moment, she felt led to utter a prayer to the heavenly Father. "Lord, I thank Thee for the progress Cecil has made in his life and especially for leading him to church this morning. I pray that Thou wilt not let him become discouraged by people who would rather talk about him than to him. Lead him to Thy way, and keep him there. And Lord, please help Aunt May see that Cecil is really not as vile as she believes. Open her heart and mind to accepting him, if that is Thy will. In the name of Jesus, amen."

At that moment, Eunice realized that she might have changed more than her student. What had happened? How had she managed to become yet another woman to be enchanted by the beguiling cad?

*

The next day, Eunice traveled to the Sutton estate with a heavy heart. Truly, Cecil had acquired the manners of royalty and had learned to enjoy reading classical literature. In her heart, she knew that her aunt was right. Cecil didn't need her anymore.

Now he is free to marry Olivia.

Eunice swallowed and clutched her throat as though she were trying to coax down a bottle of harsh elixir. Such feelings were contrary to any she expected to experience at this point. She should have been happy that her arduous task had been completed well ahead of the designated year—not only completed but finished with great success. So why did she feel as though she was a convict on the way to the gallows rather than a woman finally free of an albatross?

Could it be that you love him?

"No!" she whispered to herself and shook the thought from her mind.

She couldn't love him. She had no right. She had to think of Olivia, and she had to be obedient to Aunt May, who only had Eunice's best interests in her heart and mind—and whose wisdom and experience far exceeded Eunice's. Head held high, Eunice decided to tell Cecil that any future contact would happen only under obligatory social circumstances.

If only Cecil will tell me that he no longer wants to be with

Olivia. If only he will say he wants to be with me. An unwelcome pang of guilt shot through her at the selfish thought.

The butler answered the door. "Mrs. Sutton begs your indulgence, but she is temporarily indisposed. She has asked me to escort you to the parlor for hot tea, if that is agreeable to you."

"But of course." Such an offer held great appeal on a dreary afternoon. The gray sky seemed to cry out its raindrops.

Eunice stepped into the spacious foyer and handed the butler her wet coat. Following him, she rubbed her palms against her forearms. The motion warmed her, although she suspected the tea would be much better. Waiting in the parlor, she stood as closely to the fire as she could without endangering her dress to stray sparks. When would the tea arrive? What was taking so long?

Without warning, the silence was broken. Loud, lusty singing seemed to be coming from somewhere in the back of the house. The tunes could hardly be considered pleasant to the ear. Not only were they executed in a most off-key fashion, but the words were not the kind one would hear in church—or at most parties held in respectable homes.

Eunice shuddered. She didn't recognize the voices. Surely Tedric wasn't singing with a friend. When she listened to Cecil singing the past Sunday, he showed his insecurity in the way he fairly spoke, rather than sang, the words. Yet fear clamped her stomach.

"Please, Lord," she whispered, "let it be someone else."

Unwilling to see the songsters, she decided to stay put by the fire in the parlor, where she could feel safe from her doubts and misgivings. She stared into the orange fire, hoping that through sheer force of will, she could block out the offending noise.

An instant later, she heard the squeak of a door hinge,

followed by the clomping of feet. The off-key singers hadn't stopped their performance. Instead, they seemed to be traveling toward the parlor—toward her!

Curiosity overcoming revulsion, Eunice stepped toward the entrance of the room and peered toward the approaching voices. To her horror, she saw that Cecil and Lord Giles were walking up the hall, arms wrapped around each other's shoulders. They sang an off-key but hearty rendition of a bawdy song, a tune that Eunice had never heard. Even worse, both men still managed to hold a wine glass in one hand and a cigar in the other. Ashes from the lit tobacco fell to the floor at irregular intervals and brought the pungent odor of tobacco along with them.

Eunice wanted to run back into the parlor, to shelter by the fire in hopes she could forget the scene and convince herself, somehow, that the horror was all a figment of her overactive imagination or just a nightmare. Too shocked and appalled to move, Eunice remained in the doorway.

Lord Giles was the first to notice her. He lifted his glass in her direction. "Ah, Miss Norwood! How lovely to see you!"

Her name seemed to awaken Cecil. His eyes shot wide open, and he took his arm away from Lord Giles's shoulder with such force that Eunice wondered how he kept from setting Lord Giles's shirt on fire. The smirk Cecil wore disappeared when his jaw dropped open. "Eunice!"

"Indeed it is," Lord Giles agreed, his voice, more robust than usual, filling the large hallway. With his arm still around Cecil's shoulders, Lord Giles pushed and prodded so Cecil would walk faster toward her.

Eunice retreated into the parlor, but the men followed her.

"Why do you hurry away?" Lord Giles asked. "Do you not wish to see us? We are quite entertaining singers, as you heard."

"Yes, yes, indeed," Cecil agreed. His earlier look of remorse had disappeared. Eunice suspected that, prodded by Lord Giles, Cecil was too inebriated to realize—or to care—how silly he appeared.

"Perhaps we should try our hand in the theatre." Giles sent his companion a side-glance. "What say you, old boy?"

"I say we should give it a go."

"I suggest you listen to yourselves sing when you are sober before reaching a final conclusion regarding a change of careers," Eunice advised. She noticed that the men had removed their coats, and their shirts were rumpled. Cecil had even removed his shoes. "A ragtag company you would make, indeed."

"To be sure. We had planned to sober up by taking a walk in the rain," Lord Giles taunted her, "but methinks we might have more fun if we drink another toast."

At that moment, Eunice noticed that Lord Giles still held a half-empty glass of port, which he lifted toward her. "To the absence of that steadying force, Tedric!" He waved the glass and held it to his lips for a drink.

"Tedric," Cecil answered. "He is missing out on all the fun."

Lord Giles looked at Cecil's empty hand. "And so are you. Where is your glass, my boy?" Lord Giles asked. "Did you leave it in the study? I suggest we might fill it again, now that Miss Norwood is here."

"That is quite all right. I have no desire to have a toast made to me."

"Very well." Lord Giles rubbed his chin as if in deep thought. "I know. I shall toast you, Cecil. To our new friendship." He downed his port and wrapped his arm anew around Cecil's shoulders.

"Yes, yes. To our new friendship." Cecil nodded, then plopped into the nearest chair in a most undignified manner. "I think I've had enough for a time. Giles, old boy, you have managed to outdrink me." He raised his forefinger. "A scandal, it is. A scandal indeed."

"It is a scandal that you should be drinking at all," Eunice conveyed in her iciest tone. "I believe I shall summon the butler now. I came here to see Abigail, not to witness a drinking party. I can return another time."

"That is our misfortune," Lord Giles observed. "For if you could stay, I believe you might learn more about your gentleman scholar."

Eunice kept her face frozen in a glare.

"Look at your man now!" Lord Giles's voice held accusation and disgust. "See how well he has learned his manners!"

At that moment, Abigail descended the stairs. "Eunice! I am so sorry to keep you waiting. I—" She stopped short and looked at the two men. "Giles! Cecil! What are you doing?"

Lord Giles lifted his glass. "A toast to the lady of the manor, Abigail."

Abigail gasped and clutched her hand to her throat. "Cecil, how could you? And Giles, how could you let him?"

"You seem to believe that I have complete control over your brother-in-law, when, in fact, I do not." Lord Giles puffed his cigar.

"What are you thinking by bringing tobacco in the main hall?" Abigail admonished. "You know that smoking is not allowed anywhere in the house except the study."

"Ah, but we were in the study," Lord Giles argued. "Is that not so, Cecil?"

"It is so."

"Cecil," said Abigail, "I am deeply disappointed in you."

"But he insisted," Cecil answered. "He brought the wine, you know. I never could resist such a fine vintage—the year of my birth."

"How could you tempt him with port, Giles?" Abigail

whispered, obviously too shocked to shout in anger. "You knew how hard he was working not to drink anymore."

"Really?" Lord Giles smirked. "Once I poured him a glass of wine, he put up very little resistance. He was a bit depressed when I first arrived. Now he is much happier. Can you not see that?"

"He only seems happier. Drink, in fact, makes him miserable," Abigail answered.

"You have your opinion. I have mine." Lord Giles looked at Cecil and sneered. "As for my opinion, I like him better this way."

Eunice watched as Abigail's face grew redder than the filling of a cherry tart. "I want you out of my house this instant." Her voice loud with anger, she pointed to the door.

Lord Giles didn't make a move to obey her request. "But Abigail, I am afraid this is not your house."

"How dare you!" Abigail slapped Cecil's companion across the cheek with such force that he dropped his glass. It hit the floor and shattered, spilling its contents along with it.

"A waste of perfectly good wine, I must say," Cecil said.

"Maybe your disobedient sister-in-law is the one who needs a good slap." Lord Giles rubbed his face where her hand had made contact. A red mark was already beginning to show itself.

"More likely I would like to slap your other cheek," Eunice surprised herself with the sharp edge of her own voice.

"Now that you have managed to anger both ladies, perhaps this is a good time for you to depart, Giles," Cecil said.

"And perhaps it is a good time for me to depart, as well," Eunice said.

"But you just got here," Abigail protested.

"That is quite all right. Another day would be better."

"Please." Abigail grabbed her forearm as though the gesture

would change Eunice's mind.

"Another time," Eunice said.

"Tomorrow, then."

"Tomorrow? Abigail, you are always welcome to visit me. But because of what I witnessed here today, I am not sure I shall ever darken this door again." Eunice turned to Cecil. "Aunt May was right about you. You have not changed a bit. You never will. And to think I defended you when she told me I could not see you again."

The threat brought Cecil back to life. He jumped out of his chair, looking improper in his stocking feet, and approached Eunice. "Please, Eunice. That is not true. I have changed. I promise."

Eunice wasn't sure what to believe. Cecil's words were just what she wanted to hear, yet the stench of wine and tobacco on his breath told another story. Too upset to conduct herself with dignity, she turned and hastened out of the house, practically running for her carriage.

She had almost reached it when she felt a grip on her arm. Lord Giles was holding her cloak.

"You will get wet and cold without this. I assure you, he is not worth your death of cold."

She startled. His voice had lost all indications of slurring, and his steps had gained their solidity. The man was more despicable than ever. Clearly, chastising him would bear no fruit.

"Thank you." She jerked the coat out of his hands as she felt a torrent of tears threaten. She turned her head and refused to face him.

Lord Giles was not to be fooled. He took her by the arm and swirled her around, forcing her to look him in the eye. She tried to contort her expression into the image of pleasantness, but she knew she failed. Hot tears streamed down her cheeks.

Shock was evident on his face. "You. . .you really do love that cad!"

As much as she wanted to admit her feelings, she knew better than to answer.

Her silent admission seemed to sober him. His voice became crisp and serious. "Miss Norwood, please, I beg your forgiveness. I never meant to hurt Cecil."

"Then why did you tempt him with tobacco and alcohol?"

"I knew you would be visiting the estate today, just as you do every Monday afternoon. I wanted you to see for yourself that Cecil cannot really shake his love for drink, no matter what he says."

"The love of drink might always be a difficulty for him to overcome, but he had not touched a drop in months."

"How do you know?"

Eunice shook with doubt. In reality, since she was not by his side every second of every day, she could never know for certain. Yet Cecil had told her something that made her believe that he had a good reason never to touch a strong drink again. During the early stages of their acquaintance, Cecil had confessed to Eunice that when he first quit drinking, he fell sorely ill and had to take to his bed for a week. He refused to give her any details except to say that the experience was so awful, he never wanted to relive it. Because of his honest admission, Eunice was certain that Cecil had indeed kept his word to avoid wine. Her reasoning gave her the courage to face down Lord Giles.

"Never mind how or why I know, but I am certain." She sent him a steady gaze. "And even if he had experienced several relapses—which he has not, I assure you—there is no excuse for your behavior here today. Do you realize the damage you may have done? Do you realize you may have ruined his chances of conquering drink forever?"

Remorse flooded Lord Giles's face. "I did not mean him any harm. I am certain that a man of his strong constitution can recover quickly from this little relapse. I pray he will. He is my friend."

"Friend? How dare you call yourself his friend."

"I can see why you would think I am not a good friend to him. But Cecil had become my rival for your affections. At least, I had hoped so." Lord Giles's voice grew soft with defeat. "But now I see that he never was my rival. Long before I saw you, he had already won."

Her cheeks burned so hot that Eunice was sure they gave away her feelings.

"Your failure to answer is response enough. Never fear, Miss Norwood. You will not need to concern yourself about me any longer. I shall be going to London on business next week. I do not know when I will return. I bid you good day." He tipped his hat.

She managed to bid him a good day before disappearing into the safety of her carriage, which would take her to the sanctuary of her home.

nine

Eunice had much to contemplate on the ride back to her estate. Her mind swirled in every direction. None of the roads her thoughts traveled led to a happy destination.

So Aunt May had been right! Lord Giles had considered asking to court her. Her aunt fancied Lord Giles, heir to a sizable estate and a significant title, to be a perfect suitor. Eunice was aware that most women would have been delighted to have him court them. But not she. How could Lord Giles profess to be Cecil's friend, then try to squash him when he considered him a rival? How could he knowingly reverse all the hard work Cecil had employed in his efforts to avoid drink and tobacco?

She could never love—let alone wed—any man who could be so cruel. Let Lord Giles be some other woman's unfortunate problem. Her concern was Cecil and the consequences of his relapse.

"Father in heaven," she prayed, "I humbly implore Thee to deliver Cecil from this temptation and to keep him from yielding if he should be tempted in the future. Please help him to avoid the type of company who would ply him with temptations. I regret, Father in heaven, that I was unknowingly the cause for Cecil's strong temptation. Let me not play such a role in his future. Give him strength, oh Lord. In the name of Thy Son, Jesus Christ, amen."

Later, as she entered the house, she hoped to avoid Aunt May. Unfortunately for Eunice, her aunt bumped into her in the hallway. "What are you doing back so early?" Aunt May asked. "I thought surely you would be at Abigail's all afternoon." Obviously sensing something was amiss, she took Eunice by the forearm. "What happened? Was Cecil upset by the news that he cannot see you again?"

Eunice hesitated.

"You did tell him as you promised. Did you not?"

She couldn't look her aunt in the eye. "Not in so many words. Not yet."

"Eunice! You disappoint me."

"I beg your indulgence. But you see, he had a visitor. Lord Giles."

"Oh." Aunt May's face brightened, and she let go of Eunice's arm. "Were you and Lord Giles able to exchange pleasantries?"

Eunice thought for a moment. How could she answer without either worrying her aunt or telling a lie?

"We saw each other briefly, but there was very little time for pleasantries. I did have tea in Abigail's parlor, but then I left." She prayed her convoluted version of the afternoon's events wasn't too close to being a falsehood. She added one more observation that she knew to be the unvarnished truth. "I fear that Lord Sutton is not ready to attend any dinner we might host here. I regret to say that he may never be."

"I see," her aunt answered, although a puzzled light in her eyes indicated she wasn't sure she comprehended the situation in the least. "Then your lessons were for naught?"

"No good deed is for naught."

"You are right. Well then, why not put all this worry behind?" Aunt May suggested. "Shall both of us go to the church? I told them you would not be available to wrap bandages for the hospital, but since you are here, you may as well go and share the work and the fellowship."

Eunice was in no mood to see anyone. All she desired was to lose herself in a book or to drown her troubles in sleep. But she couldn't deny her aunt. "Will Violet be there?"

"I think so."

At least she could look forward to one bright prospect. "Very well. I shall go."

"Good. Better to spend your time in service to others than to mope around here thinking of Lord Sutton."

For the hundredth time, Eunice wished her aunt didn't know her so well. Perhaps she was right. Why should she spend all her time thinking and dreaming of something that could never be? Better to remain a spinster, valued for high service, than to be like Olivia, flitting from one beau to the next in an endless search for the perfect match—or not.

"Lord, if she marries him, let her be good to him," she whispered.

"What was that?" Aunt May asked.

"Nothing. Just a little prayer."

❧

The next day, Eunice was meeting with Cook in her study and was just about to go over the week's menu when the butler interrupted. "I beg your pardon, but Lord Sutton is here to see you, milady." He bowed and handed her Cecil's calling card.

Sitting at her desk, she stared at the card and rubbed her fingertips over the letters. She wasn't entirely surprised by the visit. Still, she wasn't sure she was ready to see him yet.

"Tell him this is not the time we are customarily at home."

"Once again I beg your pardon, milady, but he told me that he expected you to answer in such a fashion. He asked me to tell you that he is aware that he is imposing but to beg of you if he might have a moment of your time."

Eunice didn't answer right away.

"If I may be permitted to share my observations with milady?"

Her butler had proven himself an astute man. Since he had

always been trusted by Uncle Eric, Eunice knew she could place her confidence in the faithful servant, as well.

"Milady, he is dressed in a fine suit—fine enough for worship—and he shifted his weight from one foot to the other. Truly the motions of one who is nervous. I have seen many a nervous man in my day. No one conducts himself in such a manner unless his business carries significant weight."

"I suspect his business with me does carry some weight." Eunice sighed. "All right. I shall see him but only briefly."

"Shall I prepare refreshment, milady?"

"No."

The butler raised his eyebrows in obvious surprise.

Eunice knew that failing to offer Cecil any refreshment would display an indifference contrary to all the lessons she had given him, yet she couldn't bring herself to show him such hospitality. "I shall ring for you if I change my mind."

"Yes, milady." He bowed and exited.

Eunice turned her attention briefly to the cook. "If you have any leg of mutton left over from yesterday's meal, you may prepare a stew for dinner tonight if time permits."

Cook nodded. "Time permits, milady."

"I am sorry that we were interrupted here this morning. I shall see to it that we meet tomorrow to discuss the rest of the week's menu. Meet me here promptly after breakfast."

"Yes, milady." Cook curtsied and exited.

Rather than rushing to face Cecil, Eunice paused. She rose from her desk and walked about the study. Peering out of the window at the falling rain, she noticed a few new buds on the trees, a promise that spring would soon be arriving. A year had not yet passed. According to the date he had agreed upon with Olivia, Cecil still had plenty of time to reform before they became engaged. She wondered what Olivia would have thought if she had witnessed yesterday's scene. Unhappily, she supposed Olivia would have not been surprised and, if anything, might have poked fun at Eunice for being naive enough to believe that Cecil could change so easily.

Perhaps Lord Giles had done Eunice a favor by exposing Cecil as the weak individual he was. Eunice had no clear leading from God that He had chosen Cecil for her. But during her prayer time, she had never felt guidance that Cecil was not the one He had chosen for her, either. Or was yesterday's sad occurrence a confirmation that God's answer, at least this time, was no?

Please, Father in heaven, tell me why am I so confused!

Perhaps seeing Cecil would clear her head once and for all. With a heavy heart and heavier steps, she headed toward the parlor, where she knew he awaited.

When she reached the doorway, rather than entering right away, she stopped. Cecil's back was toward her. The butler had told her correctly: The suit he wore fit him to perfection. Apparently he had purchased it in London and had it tailored to flatter his slimmer physique. He was staring out of the window, just as she had stared out of her study window moments before. What was he thinking?

As though he sensed her presence, he turned and faced her. "Eunice. You have my utmost gratitude for agreeing to see me today." He strode to her. With his usual fanfare, he lifted her hand so her palm faced upward and swept his warm lips across her wrist. Why did the gesture always have to send shivers of pleasure through her body?

She tried to keep her tone even, although she wasn't sure she succeeded. "The butler said you indicated that your business is of some importance."

"Yes."

She knew he was waiting for her to take a seat so he could

follow suit. Whatever he had to say, he apparently planned to take more than a moment. Bringing her light shawl closer to her neck, she regretted that she hadn't asked the butler to be sure the fire was adequate and that she had turned down his suggestion that he make tea. She took a seat on the sofa. To her surprise, Cecil was bold enough to sit directly beside her. He was so close that she could smell the pleasant bay rum scent of his shaving lotion. She tried not to let herself become distracted by his presence.

She could see by the trouble he had taken with his appearance, by the remorseful look on his face, and by the timing of his visit that he sought her absolution. She could forgive him as commanded by her Christian duty. But could she ever meet him in a crowd again and see him as just another acquaintance? No. She could not. She braced herself for the courage to deliver the bad news. But before she spoke, she owed him the courtesy of listening to his plea.

"First," he said, "I must compliment you and your aunt on the fine progress you have made in decorating this parlor. I haven't seen South Hampton look so fine—not even at the height of its glory."

Though he spoke in hyperbole, Eunice appreciated his words all the same. "Thank you, but I am afraid the glory stops here. Should you tour the rest of the house, you might be disappointed. We still have much work to do. Aunt May and I have chosen our color schemes for the rest of the rooms, but we must wait for the weather to clear before we can make serious progress in repainting or putting up new wallpaper."

He looked toward the window. "Yes, we have been experiencing our share of rain lately."

Eunice paused. "I know you did not come here to speak of our new decorations or to talk about the weather."

"True. And I should not impose on your time when you

were gracious enough to receive me without an invitation." He paused, then cleared his throat. "I feel I must speak with you about yesterday."

"There is no need. Lord Giles already explained."

"Explained what?"

Eunice was sorry that she blurted out her thoughts before considering the consequences. "You mean, you have no idea what happened yesterday?"

"I know that I behaved abominably."

"But you have no idea why Lord Giles tempted you?"

He thought for a moment. "Giles is known to have a liking for fine tobacco and a glass of wine now and again. And since Monday is Tedric's usual day to go into the village on errands, Giles knew that my priggish brother would not be present to object if we indulged a bit."

"Apparently neither of you gave a thought to Abigail," she reminded him. "Or to little Cecilia."

"Cecilia is too young to understand much about what happens outside her little world in the nursery."

"As it should be," Eunice added.

"Yes. As it should be." He cast his stare to the rug. "I wish I had considered Abigail before I imbibed. I thought one glass would not hurt, but Giles kept offering me one glass after another. I remembered how much I enjoyed such a fine wine. I—I suppose I took leave of my better judgment."

"So it appeared." Eunice kept her voice gentle.

"Eunice, I behaved in a most detestable fashion. I beg your forgiveness."

"Has Abigail forgiven you?"

"Would my answer have any effect on yours?"

"No," she admitted, "but I do hope you apologized to her. You may own Sutton Manor, but she is the lady of the house. She is the one you embarrassed with your behavior, not I."

"Yes, I realize that. I never should have shown such disrespect for her—or for Tedric. And yes, I have begged forgiveness from both of them. They say they are willing to put the matter aside, yet I know from their frosty attitude that they are still licking their wounds."

"Only because they care so much about you."

"But I must ask—you seem to think Giles had some reason for tempting me. Why?"

"My opinion is of no consequence. I am more interested in helping you make amends with Abigail."

"Thank you, but I will not be so easily distracted." He thought for a moment. "I remember now. Giles ran after you with your cloak. He talked to you for some time. What did he say?"

"I have no reason to think he will be bringing drink and tobacco to your house again."

"He told you that?"

"I think he realizes he hampered your progress. I think he is truly sorry about that. And he sees no reason to repeat his action."

"No reason, eh?" Cecil's eyes widened as if a light had been lit in his brain. "I think I know what you are talking about. He wanted to lower your opinion of me, did he not?"

Eunice hesitated. How could she answer?

"Your silence is answer enough. I see everything clearly now. He shoved me aside in church so he could sit in your pew. I should have seen that as a clear indication that he wanted to ask to court you. So, Eunice, did he succeed?"

"Succeed at what?"

"His attempt to court you. Is that what he was inquiring about when he took you your cloak? He wanted to inquire if he could approach your aunt for permission to court you?"

"Even if he did, I would never accept such a proposal from

a man with an excess of wine on his breath."

"So he did broach the subject of your courtship."

"No. He realized. . ." Eunice paused. She wanted to finish her sentence, but she couldn't. To tell Cecil everything that Lord Giles told her would be to reveal her feelings for Cecil. And she couldn't do that. Not now. Not ever.

"He realized what?" Cecil asked.

"That. . .that courting me would be impossible."

Cecil narrowed his eyes as if he were contemplating whether or not to pursue the line of discussion. Eunice sent him a stern look meant to discourage him. Thankfully, it worked.

"At this moment, my concern is not Giles," he finally said. "My concern is you. I never meant to hurt you, Eunice. You have been so faithful a friend to me all this time. You never judged me. You have always been a true friend. A better friend than any man I can think of at the moment—certainly better than that rogue Giles. You truly have shown yourself to be a far better friend than I ever deserved."

Friend. Friend. Friend. The word kept echoing in her mind. That was all she was to Cecil, a friend. A treasured friend, if his flowery compliments were to be believed. But only a friend, nevertheless.

"And though I do not deserve your lightest consideration, I pray you will indulge me with your forgiveness. I truly have no notion as to why I was so weak. I promise not to give in to temptation in the future. Will you please, please forgive me?"

For a moment, Eunice wondered if Cecil planned to get down on his knees. She decided she should answer before he took such drastic action. "Of course I forgive you, Cecil. But my forgiveness is not what is important. Can you forgive yourself?"

He looked puzzled. "Forgive myself? The thought never occurred to me."

"Of course you should. Surely you know the consequences you will suffer for your setback. Now that you have given in once, perhaps resisting next time will be even more difficult. And there will be a next time for temptation. There always is."

With a gentle motion, he took the tip of her chin into the cusp of his fingers. "How did you become so wise, my little dove?"

A harsh voice interrupted. "Eunice! What is the meaning of this?"

ten

"Aunt May!" Eunice said as she rose from her seat. She noticed that Cecil quickly followed suit. "I did not hear you come in."

"That fact is obvious. I thought I told you not to see this gentleman."

"I beg your forgiveness," Cecil said. "I assume all the responsibility for my presence here."

"I see that my niece has been successful in teaching you your manners." Aunt May sneered at Cecil. "I heard you say that you think my niece is wise."

"Indeed." He kept his expression kind. "Wise beyond her years."

"Then she certainly did not gain wisdom from dillydallying with the likes of you."

"Aunt May!" Eunice blurted. "How could you say such a thing to my guest?"

"Your guest? As I have just said, I did not give you permission to entertain Cecil, the Earl of Sutton, as your guest." She nearly spat out the words. "And as your guardian, I am entitled to say anything I like to a man of whom I do not approve."

"Do not approve?" Hurt was evident in Cecil's voice. He cast his gaze to the rug. "I suppose with my reputation, I deserve your disdain."

Aunt May gave him a hard-eyed stare. "Indeed."

His blue eyes met her brown ones. "I beg your indulgence. I did not seek her attentions, except as a friend and tutor."

"Friend, indeed!" She waved her fan at them in a scolding motion. "I am of the opinion that men and women cannot be friends. There is always an element of romantic intrigue. If none is present, they lose interest in one another quickly."

"Are you saying you have no friends who are men?" Eunice asked. "And are you really so cynical, Auntie?"

"To answer your first query, no. I am acquainted with a number of gentlemen, but since I am a woman, I do not share the sort of friendship with them that I enjoy with other women. And as for my cynicism, I prefer to think of myself as wise. My wisdom is gained from living on this earth longer than either of you. Heed my words. And speaking of words," she added, "just what were the two of you discussing when I entered?"

"Nothing," they answered in unison.

"A simultaneous and fast denial can only mean intrigue as thick as clotted cream."

"Oh, Auntie, you are so amusing."

"Old ladies in their dotage usually are." She fanned herself despite the chill in the room. Undeterred, she plopped herself in the rocker and began moving back and forth. Eunice knew by the way she settled into her seat that she would take the discussion to the bitter end. "Now humor me and tell me what is going on. As your guardian, I ask that you keep no secrets from me."

Cecil responded. "I promise that my intentions toward your niece are nothing less than honorable. I admire and respect her more than any other woman of my acquaintance."

"No doubt she deserves your admiration and respect more than any other woman of your acquaintance."

"If I may respectfully remind you, Auntie, my friend Abigail is his sister-in-law."

"Even Abigail pales in comparison to you, Eunice," Cecil said.

Eunice swallowed. What could she say to such a compliment? Aunt May pointed her finger in the air. "See? That is exactly what I mean. I come in here and interrupt a conversation on forgiveness, only to have you both deny you were talking about anything, and now you are saying Eunice is superior to her godly friend. And you would have me believe that there is no intrigue between you?"

"I was merely trying to salvage what might be left of our friendship," Cecil protested. "You see, I behaved badly yesterday, and Eunice was unfortunate to witness the worst of it."

"Impossible. Eunice does not frequent gaming halls. How dare you insinuate that she should see you in a state of drunkenness."

"I beg your most kind indulgence," Cecil said. "I did not mean to imply for a moment that Miss Norwood would even consider patronizing anything but the most upstanding and respectable establishments. No, my deed was even more shameful. I indulged myself in the confines of my own home, knowing full well that my sister-in-law and my dear little niece—my namesake Cecilia—were present elsewhere in the house. I am truly ashamed of my behavior." His downturned lips and sad eyes confirmed his feelings.

"But you are not entirely to blame," Eunice couldn't help but note. "Lord Giles tempted you on purpose so I would see you fall."

"Did he?"

Eunice nodded. "He admitted so himself."

Aunt May's eyebrows shot up. "There, Lord Sutton. Surely you will be man enough to step aside and allow a worthy man, Lord Giles, to court Eunice. After all, you are on the brink of an engagement yourself."

Eunice watched Cecil swallow. "You did not tell me this before."

"I–I . . ."

Cecil's mouth twisted into an unhappy line. "Of course. He

knew Tedric would be away in the village and that you were supposed to come by and give me another lesson. He deliberately tempted me with wine and tobacco so I would appear to be badly behaved in front of you. Why, that rogue!"

"May I remind you, Lord Sutton, that you are in the presence of ladies?" Aunt May said. "That will be enough of such foul language."

"I beg your pardon, Lady May. And yours as well, Miss Norwood." He sighed. "If this were my grandfather's day, a trick such as the one Giles employed on me would have been enough to challenge him to a duel."

"Thankfully, this is not your grandfather's day. A duel would solve nothing and leave you both wounded or worse," Eunice observed. "Please try to hold back your anger. I understand why you feel betrayed. You have every right to feel that you could trust a friend. And Lord Giles, by his treachery, has proven that he is not your friend."

"Friend or not, he accepted wine from Lord Giles," Aunt May said.

"And I was a cad to do so. I never should have taken the first drop." Cecil turned pleading eyes toward Eunice. "Eunice, I beg you to forgive me."

Eunice never could resist Cecil when he looked at her with those blue eyes. "Of course I can forgive you."

"And what about the next time—and the next?" Aunt May asked.

"There will be no next time," Cecil assured her.

"Really?" Aunt May persisted. "What evidence can you provide to show me that I should trust you?"

"I realize my reputation is not the best, but I am trying to improve. I had given up strong drink and tobacco for nearly six months before yesterday."

Aunt May gasped. "How is anyone to know you have not

resumed your bad habits altogether?"

"I have not."

"I believe him," Eunice confirmed. "You are near enough to observe for yourself that there is no odor of tobacco stench upon his clothing. Nor is there a hint of drink upon his breath."

"Agreed." Aunt May looked at the clock on the mantel. "Yet it is only ten in the morning. The day is young."

"And the day shall draw to a close without my becoming intoxicated or lighting a cigar of any kind," Cecil promised.

"How you spend your time, whether sober or inebriated, is no concern of mine," Aunt May said in disgust. "Unless. . ." She turned her eyes toward Eunice. "He said you witnessed the worst of his behavior."

"I am afraid so."

"When he was drunk, did Lord Sutton offend you in any way?"

"Oh, no, Aunt May. I–I mean, his singing was enough to make a dog howl, but he never laid a hand on me or tried to kiss me—"

"Eunice!" Aunt May waved her fan as furiously as though she were trying to ward off the heat of an afternoon in deep summer.

"Forgive me." She felt her face flush hot. "That is what you meant, is it not?"

"I suppose, but you know a lady never utters such intimate concerns aloud!" She stomped her foot and turned to Cecil. "You have been nothing but a poor influence on my niece ever since the day you set eyes upon her. Despite your title and your position as the eldest son of a fine family, she has no business involving herself with the likes of you. Did you know that Eunice was not visiting Sutton Manor today in order to give you another etiquette lesson?"

"No, Lady May. I assumed she planned to give me a lesson."

"She did not. I had instructed her to tell you that you are forbidden to see her again. I told her to write a letter, but she wanted to tell you herself, in person. I knew then that such kind consideration was more than you deserved, but I gave in to her wishes, knowing her tender heart. And to think that she found you in a drunken state! No wonder she was unable to tell you my verdict. Well, I shall tell you now in no uncertain terms. I forbid you to see my niece in the future. Am I understood?"

Cecil looked into Aunt May's eyes. For an instant, it seemed as though he planned to argue. Yet Aunt May, though short and plump and wearing a frock fashioned of a light gray wool, looked like a warship ready to shoot its cannons. Eunice knew that debating her was a useless exercise when she had worked herself up to such a state. She was thankful that Cecil could apparently draw the same conclusion.

"I understand, Lady May, and I will respect your wishes."

"Good. You must understand that this means that Miss Norwood will not be visiting Sutton Manor in the future. There will be no more etiquette lessons for you." She sniffed. "Although no doubt, you could certainly use plenty more."

"I know I have no right to ask any favors of you, but if you could consider granting me one—not for myself, but for your niece—I would be grateful," Cecil implored. "Please do not forbid her to visit the estate. I will make good on my promise to keep myself in another wing of the house during Miss Norwood's visits. I do not wish for my foolish lapse in judgment to interfere with the conviviality that Eunice and Abigail enjoy."

Aunt May thought for a moment. "Do you promise?"

"Yes. You have my word as an earl."

She scrutinized him for a moment before reaching her decision. "Then I will take you at your word."

Cecil nodded to her aunt, then sent Eunice the curt nod she would expect from a mere acquaintance. At that moment, she realized how much she had enjoyed her easy camaraderie with Cecil. She knew she would miss him more than she could say.

"Well!" Aunt May said as soon as the door shut behind Cecil. "Good riddance. Let his feet never darken our door again."

"Did you have to be so harsh, Aunt May?"

"Indeed I did! I heard what he said about Lord Giles. I was right! He does want to court you! Now there is not a thing to hold you back. With my verdict in place, Lord Sutton cannot lay the slightest claim upon you. Oh, what a joyous day this is for the Norwoods. Your uncle would be so proud of your prospects here."

"Yes, Auntie." Eunice knew her voice held little enthusiasm. She didn't have the heart to tell her aunt that she had spurned Lord Giles without so much as a morsel of regret or that he was clearly aware that she had no interest in being courted by him—ever.

"Now our little dinner party has become even more urgent," Aunt May said. "We must hurry to decorate the house. Just last Sunday, the brigadier general was asking us when we planned to open the house. Once we are ready, he will be so pleased."

"No more pleased than you, I can see." In spite of the awfulness of the day, Eunice was nevertheless happy to see her aunt enjoy the prospect of entertaining. As they became well acquainted with more people in the parish, the list of invitees had grown. Each name added increased Aunt May's anticipation.

If only Cecil could be a part of their evening. But he could not. Not after her aunt had spurned him.

Lord, she prayed in silence, *I know Aunt May wants what is best for me. Please give me the strength to obey her guidance with the utmost cheerfulness. In the precious name of Thy Son, amen.*

❧

Over the next few weeks, Eunice visited Abigail more than usual. To her disappointment, Cecil kept his word and never so much as entered the room where she and Abigail shared tea. She had taught him how to be a gentleman. Too well, it would seem.

Eunice confided the news of her aunt's edict to her friend. Abigail commiserated but offered no alternative or aid in changing her aunt's mind. Eunice always inquired after him and, to her comfort, received glowing reports that he was keeping away from his forbidden habits. Abigail told Eunice she could claim victory in how she had aided Cecil's change of lifestyle. What little reward, when she could never look upon his face, hear his voice, or relish his nearness. As she entered and exited her carriage, she surveyed the yard and windows of the manor house, hoping to see him even from a distance, even for a moment. But her efforts were in vain.

She missed him. More than she had ever missed anyone before in her life. And there was not a thing she could do to change the situation.

❧

Cecil heard the clapping of horses' hooves against the drive.

"Who could that be?" They weren't expecting any visitors. For an instant, his heart beat with hope. Could it be Eunice?

So what if it were? A visit from Eunice would only mean he would be required to dash up the stairs to the solitude of his room, where he could be neither seen nor heard.

He sighed. He had agreed to keep under wraps during her visits and, so far, he had managed to keep his word. From his lonely room upstairs, he could hear Abigail and Eunice laughing as they took tea like two of the happiest schoolgirls in all of England. Just hearing her voice tortured him when he could not see her or speak with her even in a casual greeting. After each of her visits, Cecil queried Abigail about her—what she wore, how robust she appeared, what she had to say. Abigail always reported that Eunice inquired after him. It was a small comfort, but he accepted her interest as the best he could do for the time being. Or forever.

He wished he had never made such a preposterous agreement to stay out of Eunice's sight. What had he been thinking? A rash statement, to be sure, to appease an angry aunt.

"Father in heaven," he prayed. "Help me to stop reacting with my emotions rather than my reason."

A few weeks ago, he wouldn't have uttered a prayer, and certainly not one so impromptu. Yet since he had kept abreast of his Bible reading, Cecil had begun to consult the Lord more often. A change in his general attitude and outlook on life quickly followed suit.

He wished Eunice could see him now. Rather than setting him back and leading him down the road to drink, Cecil's error with Giles had only firmed his resolve not to relapse.

But since he had made the promise, he knew he would have to disappear should his visitor be Eunice. He peered out of the parlor window. As soon as he saw the carriage, he readily identified his visitor.

"Olivia."

eleven

What was Olivia doing here? Why had she journeyed all the way from London? The year was not quite up, so surely the purpose of her visit wasn't to stake her claim to him.

Cecil watched her emerge from the carriage. Elegant as always, she wore a soft muslin frock. The dress was cut more daringly than it should have been for daytime, but whether the time be day or night, Olivia was never one to shy away from displaying her well-formed figure. The bright yellow color of the fabric and feathered hat did wonders for her complexion and set off her brown hair. She made a pretty sight, indeed. Whatever her reasons for making the trip, they were important, as clearly her manner of dress was calculated to get his attention.

Yet without making a conscious effort to do so, he imagined Eunice wearing such a dress. Even though she would never consider such a daring cut, she would certainly have appeared just as stunning—even more so. He remembered the first night he had seen Eunice, at the ball in London. She had been wearing a cast-off dress of Olivia's. Even then she shone above all the other women. Now that she was home and privy to her own seamstress, Eunice always appeared in flattering yet modest clothing in colors meant to suit her blond complexion and creamy skin.

He tried to shake the image of Eunice out of his head. What was the matter with him? He had no right to think about her, especially with Olivia just steps away from his front door.

Forcing himself to concentrate on unanticipated business,

he decided he should try to look his best. Cecil rushed up the stairs to his room so he could freshen up quickly before greeting her. At the top of the landing, he nearly bumped into Luke in his haste.

"Good. There you are. I was just about to ring for you."

"Yes, milord?"

"We have an unexpected visitor—Lady Olivia Hamilton. Have tea prepared for her and escort her into the parlor. I shall be available to greet her in but a moment."

"Yes, milord."

Once he had arrived in the shelter of his room, Cecil inspected his reflection in the mirror. Thankfully, he had shaved recently enough so that no new beard growth was evident. Since he wouldn't be wearing a hat while indoors, he smoothed his hair and made sure each strand was in place. He splashed on a bit of bay rum scent and allowed Luke to assist him into a frock coat suitable for the afternoon. The blue tie he had donned earlier that day still had not become rumpled. He brushed off his boots and, with one final look in the mirror, decided he cut a dashing figure, indeed. He was ready to see Olivia.

As he descended the stairs, he heard Abigail chatting with his visitor. Their voices sounded pleasant enough. Apparently Olivia, known to be flighty and easily offended, had not come in a fit of rage over some imagined slight. He exhaled a sigh of relief.

He puffed out his chest and entered the room with a confident stride. "Good morning, Abigail." He nodded.

"Good morning."

He set his sights on the picture in yellow. "Olivia, my dear. How lovely to see you." He lifted her wrist to his lips. His gallant gesture usually caused Eunice's soft hands to tremble with obvious delight. Olivia gave him no discernible response.

"Oh, good," Abigail noted. "Here is the tea."

"Will you not stay?" Cecil asked.

"Thank you, but no. I am taking tea with Tedric in the study." Abigail tilted her head toward Olivia. "I hope you will be staying for dinner?"

"Yes, by your leave."

"But of course." She smiled and departed.

Olivia didn't delay in settling herself into the red upholstered wing chair that was Cecil's comfortable favorite. She looked about the room, surveying the carved ceiling, the wallpaper that depicted dancing couples, the hardwood floors, and the patterned Oriental rug, as though she were already the mistress of the manor. "My, but I hardly remember the last time I visited here. It has been so long. Too long," Olivia said. "This place has not changed at all. I rather feel as though I am coming home."

"Indeed? After living in London all your life, I imagine you would find the country boring after only a week."

She looked around the room once more. "A woman can change her mind, you know."

Cecil felt uneasy. The references to feeling at home and changing her mind were certain to foreshadow news for him—unwelcome news at that. He watched the woman he was supposed to marry as she sipped her tea. He knew many of his friends married for expediency rather than love, but he was in a social and financial position to choose a suitable wife from an array of aristocratic women. Suddenly, he knew why he had been a bachelor all these years. No woman—including Olivia—had made him experience any feelings beyond pleasant companionship. Until he met Eunice.

He listened only with half an ear as Olivia prattled about the latest gossip from their friends and foes in London. Her tongue was sweet when speaking about those who were popular or for whom she had some fondness. The same tongue became bitter when she referred to her rivals. Her news was a listing of which parties were grandest, which women were dressed the most fashionably, and who spurned whom or who loved whom.

Months ago, he would have found such scandal broth amusing. He might even have cheered for the winners and rejoiced in the defeats of those he didn't favor. But today, as Olivia spoke on and on, he realized that very little she had to say was of any interest to him.

He couldn't help but notice that her monologue avoided mention of one London resident in particular. "Tell me, Olivia," he asked, "how is Lord George?"

"George?" Olivia's mouth dropped open slightly. Her hand trembled so that her cup and saucer rattled. The tinkling noise reverberated throughout the room. "Fine."

"Really? You seem distressed."

"I have nothing to be distressed about, especially not regarding him." Her shrill tone belied her words.

"Tedric journeys into the village each Monday to do weekly errands. Often, he hears gossip floating about. Even news from London."

Olivia, who had just taken a portion of biscuit, coughed so that she spewed a few crumbs from her mouth. She recovered and patted her lips with her napkin. "Pardon me. Now, you were saying you heard news from London all the way out here?"

"Of course. You know how quickly rumors fly." He leaned forward. "So can you tell me, is there any truth to the rumor that Lord George Loughton became betrothed to his distant cousin not a fortnight ago?"

"Yes. It is true. The marriage is not a love match. They will be combining their estates, keeping them both in the Loughton family line. I think under the circumstances, he has made a—a wise. . .decision."

For a moment, he almost felt sorry for Olivia. So she really did love that dog after all. He wanted to reach over and pat her hand but realized that she had been playing him for a fool. And he had fallen willingly into her trap.

"Perhaps a change of subject is in order. Tell me Olivia," he said, "what have you been reading lately?"

She shrugged. "Nothing of consequence."

"Since I have been home, I have begun a fascinating study of my father's books. I am currently comparing the philosophies of Plato and Socrates. Did you know that Socrates believed that no human agent knowingly does wrong?"

"No."

"Plato disagreed, saying that weakness of will can interfere with moral conduct."

"Oh. That is quite interesting, I am sure. But I have no idea what you think those philosophies have to do with me. Are you implying that I am weak willed or that I knowingly do wrong?"

"Of course not. I was merely sharing what I have been reading."

"If you say so. My mother taught me to be a lady and to leave discussions of problems that have no solution to men with nothing better to do than to discuss them, trying to make others believe they are superior in their knowledge." She let out an exasperated sigh. "Really, Cecil, I thought you came here to hunt. Have you nothing better to do?"

Nothing better to do. Eunice had not responded with such disdain when he had asked her about Socrates and his student, Plato. The very topic had resulted in a lively discussion that lasted most of the afternoon. Not that he could blame Olivia for her lack of interest. Admittedly, women were not usually encouraged to think about the unanswerable questions philosophy could pose. Eunice had admitted a love for solitude during her school years, and he pictured her as a girl with her nose stuck in a book. Her studies had resulted in a finely tuned grasp of the classics. While she didn't pretend to know all the answers, she offered excellent insights and opinions that were informed and entertaining. He realized that Eunice had spoiled him. He now expected every woman to be equipped for intelligent discourse.

"Indeed," he answered, "I think I have spent my time wisely."

"Prodded by my little cousin, no doubt."

"Eunice?"

"That is right. I heard about your so-called etiquette lessons." She threw him a knowing smile. "Just as you say news travels from London to the country, remember, the news travels from the country to London just as rapidly."

"Who told you?"

"Eunice. . .and Giles."

"Giles." He nodded. "I might have known." He patted his napkin against his mouth with several quick motions, then set it again in his lap. Rather than letting go, he crinkled the cloth in his hands.

Apparently his nervousness didn't go unnoticed. "Why does my knowledge upset you? Unless you are too weak-willed to keep from doing what you know to be wrong. . . Is that why you are studying philosophy? To find an excuse for your failings?"

"Not at all. I seek no excuse, but I hope to improve. Just as you asked me to." He leaned toward her. "Remember?"

She bristled, then drew back, reminding him of a cat ready to defend herself against an angered hunting dog. "Of course I remember. Why else do you believe I came here today?"

"Oh, is that the reason for your visit? I find it interesting that you chose to grace us with your presence without so much as a letter advising us to expect you. Were you hoping to find me in error?" Now back in control, he smoothed his napkin on his lap.

"No. Of course not. And from the looks of you, I think I would be hard pressed to find you drinking or smoking. Or even overeating. I notice you seem thinner than when we last met."

"An improvement, I hope?"

"I suppose you do look better." Her tone indicated that he would never look handsome in her eyes.

"Now that you have seen me again and conducted your surprise inspection, I trust you are satisfied that I will be able to meet your requirements by our agreed-upon date?"

"Yes, I am quite satisfied. In the past, you had normally consumed several glasses of wine by this time in the afternoon. I am pleased to find you sober."

"Then by all accounts, your inspection has been a success, although I trust you will be staying this evening."

"I plan to do more than that. I plan to stay several weeks." She paused, obviously to give him time to process this tidbit of news.

"Several weeks?"

"Yes." She smiled in triumph. "It is time to plan our wedding. I want to marry right away."

Cecil didn't know how to respond. "Right away? In a matter of months, you mean."

"No. In a matter of one month at most."

One month? This was the moment he had been waiting for—Olivia's willingness, no, eagerness, to marry. He searched his heart to find an inch of excitement. He found none. Not even an iota of anticipation. Only a strange sort of fear. Why?

He could only stall by asking her questions. "Why the change of heart? First you wanted me to wait a year. Now you are not looking forward to the prospect of waiting a day. This sudden change is not like you, Olivia."

"As I said, a woman is entitled to change her mind."

Cecil thought for a moment. Olivia never reacted irrationally unless she felt threatened or abandoned. Now that George had committed to someone else, that would explain her feelings of abandonment. But who would be a threat? He thought back to moments before and realized that she had mentioned the woman she feared most—Eunice.

"I will grant you that. But this sudden uge to marry isn't like you, Olivia," he pointed out.

She shrugged. The motion, obviously meant to be casual, seemed contrived. "Oh, I do not know. Perhaps I thought a wedding just after Easter would be lovely." She waved her head in a coy manner.

"Perhaps." He paused, hoping for elaboration.

"The spring is so pretty with fresh blossoms everywhere."

"A date that close wouldn't give us much time to be engaged."

"But it would give us plenty of time to prepare. I have the perfect dress in mind." Olivia chattered on about commissioning her seamstress for a dress dripping in lace and pearls, but Cecil took in few of the other details. He was too shocked by her sudden change.

"Cecil!" Her sharp tone interrupted his thoughts. "Have you heard a word I said?"

"I cannot promise to quote you directly, no."

"But you must know about the catering. I just attended the Williamses' wedding, and the ceremony and reception were quite stupendous. You should have seen the food. George could not stop praising each delicacy."

"George? You went to the Williamses' wedding with George?" His voice was an octave higher than usual.

Her face fell, taking on a look of guilt. "Did I not mention that?"

"You mentioned you had no plans to attend—in one of the

few letters I have received from you," he added.

"You know I never was one to keep up a warm correspondence. And I suppose I did not want to bother you with journeying all the way to London when you were enjoying yourself here in the country."

"Or perhaps you thought I was not yet ready to escort you to an event of such importance," he deduced. "You will be happy to learn that I have made considerable progress not only in improving my bad habits but in recalling all the niceties I learned in the past and refining them to perfection. Just ask Miss Norwood."

She rose to her feet, nearly knocking over what remained of the tea and biscuits. "Eunice! Eunice! Eunice! I am so sick and tired of hearing nothing but Eunice! Eunice! Eunice! First from Giles, and now from you. I wish I had never heard the name of my little country cousin!"

"Giles?" Jealousy roared through Cecil. He threw his napkin on the table and stood up to face Olivia. "What did Giles say about Eunice?"

Olivia crossed her arms and glared at him. "Oh, nothing much. Just how she had broken his heart."

"How absurd! Why, she never even so much as gave him a second look."

"But he had eyes for her. And he told me that instead of contemplating courtship with an eligible bachelor, she had set her sights on you!"

"That is even more absurd. I admit we developed a fondness for one another during our lessons and discussions, but Eunice would never consider me as a suitor. She knew she was teaching me manners only so I could become betrothed to you."

"My question is, why did Eunice have to teach you manners? Certainly your sister-in-law, Abigail, could have done the job."

"You know the history Abigail and I share. I think she made the right choice to ask her friend to take me on."

"So her friend could steal you away?"

"She did not steal me away. If you want to place blame on anyone, look in the mirror." He tilted his head toward the large gilded mirror that hung beside the window on the north wall.

She took his advice. He watched Olivia appraise herself. "Anyone can plainly see that I am no longer as young as Eunice." She cocked her head. "But I am still attractive. And I have connections. Why, I am the most popular hostess in London!" She turned back to him, eyes narrowed. "How could you even consider her?"

"Who says I am?"

"Giles, of course. And your fit of rage at the mention of his name confirms the suspicions he expressed to me."

"You listen to the ramblings of a lovesick puppy. Pay him no heed."

"So you say, but I am not so sure. If you really want to prove Giles wrong and put to rest any rumors that might be circulating about the three of us, you will agree to an Easter wedding." She nodded once as though her declaration would settle the matter.

He didn't have to think before making his decision. "I will not."

Her eyes widened and took on a light he seldom saw in them. Fear, perhaps? "A month later, then," she suggested.

"No."

"June?" Her features hardened. "The wedding must take place no later than in the spring."

"I am sorry, Olivia, but I have no idea why you are hurrying to set a wedding date. We are not formally betrothed as of yet. And I am not sure at this moment that I wish to prolong our courtship."

Olivia gasped. "What! How dare you! How dare you reject me for that. . .that. . ." She pointed an accusing finger in the general direction of South Hampton Manor.

"Although I regard Eunice highly, do not blame her. She is not the one who caused me to lose my love for you."

"Then who?"

"You did." Speaking the words aloud made him realize the truth they held. "You took your love away from me bit by bit. First, by putting conditions on our betrothal."

"And you are looking all the better for it."

"I must admit, I am feeling in much better health, although I do miss my wine. But that is not all. You have humiliated me by cavorting with that dog, George."

"And a dog he is, too. You have no reason to feel humiliated. You were out of town," she pointed out. "But George is neither here nor there. I am not going to lose again. I want you to come back to London with me today. London is where you belong, with me."

"Why this sudden desire to wed at all? I thought you liked your freedom. At least, that is what you told Eunice."

Olivia blanched. "What else did she tell you?"

"Nothing. Just that she admired your independent spirit."

"Oh, really?" Her voice dripped with doubt.

"I give you my word as a lord and a son of the empire, Eunice never said a negative word about you. Even though she admitted she does not know you well, she spoke of you with the highest regard. Perhaps, my dear, that is precisely why she spoke so well of you."

"How dare you! Why, if you were any other man, I–I would—"

"Slap me across the cheek? It would not be the first time." Cecil couldn't help but remember his first encounter with Eunice, when she had spurned his kiss with a sound slap that echoed through the garden.

"So she never told you that I—" Olivia stopped herself short.

"Told me what? That you do not really love me at all?"

Olivia couldn't meet his gaze.

"You did not need Eunice to betray a confidence. As you should be able to deduce, I had already come to that conclusion on my own."

"If you think you can have Eunice, think again. How can you be happy living here in the country all the time, with nothing to do but hunt and fish? I will admit readily that I am not as pure as your Eunice. She reminds me of a nun with her piousness. If you indeed chose not to marry me, never in a lifetime would I have chosen Eunice as a match for you. We are two of a kind, you know. Irresponsible, selfish, reckless. Unrepentant sinners. I assure you, living with Eunice would be your worst nightmare."

"But that is where you are wrong. I would be happy with someone like Eunice. For I am no longer an unrepentant sinner. I have come to know the Savior."

Olivia sneered. "So you say, just to pacify her, no doubt. But I doubt your so-called faith can sustain you when you face the one temptation you never speak of—even to me. Yes, I know about her. Lizzie."

A small gasp escaped his lips.

"You thought I never knew? I know more than you think."

Shame flooded him. "I had no idea. I was a cad. I never meant to cause you such anguish."

"Do you think you are the only man with such an arrangement? The gossips are only too happy to let us know as many details as they can."

A wave of protectiveness swept over him. He wanted to console the woman he had hurt. He strode over to her and reached out his arms for an embrace.

She twirled out of his reach. "You think I am so fragile that I will break into pieces if I discover the way the world works? I am not. But Eunice is. As you no doubt have seen, she does not go to church for appearances as some of us do. She truly is a Christian, and despite being orphaned and pawned off on an uncle at an early age, she has lived a very sheltered life. She has just inherited a grand house and enough money to keep her protected from the underworld. I doubt she has even heard of the likes of Lizzie. Gambling, drunkenness, debauchery. What will she think?" A laugh escaped Olivia's lips, but the sound was not pretty.

Cecil shuddered.

"Do you really believe that Eunice could overlook your past? Could she believe your vow to change your ways? I think not."

Other than to stop pacing, Cecil didn't answer. How could he argue?

"I, on the other hand, am more than happy to overlook your diversions."

"You put up a brave front, but in reality, I think you would prefer a husband who would never think of patronizing a gaming hall. And I want you to know, I have not seen Lizzie or gambled in months and never plan to do so again."

"Indeed? Then why was your carriage parked in front of her house the same night you visited me in London?"

She certainly hadn't exaggerated about the gossips. He held back a grimace. "I admit, I instructed the driver to take me there. But once I arrived, I discovered that I had no desire to join the party. I immediately went to see you instead."

"I suppose I should be flattered, but I am not. You never thought of giving up anything for me before I asked—no, demanded it. But you are willing to give up everything you consider amusing for Miss Norwood?"

"Your query deserves an answer." Yet he didn't respond right away. Instead, he thought for a moment. True, he had started out giving up his bad habits to please Olivia, but only because she forced his hand. So why was it so much easier to resist temptation now? At that moment, Cecil realized why. "Olivia, I have come to the happy conclusion that the things I once called 'amusing' no longer are."

"But how can that be? You enjoyed all those things for years."

"And you wanted to take them away from me. You thought I would fail, did you not? You thought I would never be able to give up every undesirable habit I had acquired over the years. That would have given you an excuse to go to Loughton. Am I right?"

"Do not be absurd." The guilt on her face told another story.

Cecil could only look upon Lady Olivia, a part of that past life, with pity. How could she ever have a happy and satisfying relationship when she was so obviously willing to settle for seconds?

"Olivia, you deserve better than me. Do not settle for a marriage based on a relationship where the love has withered. Go back to London and find yourself a man who loves you so deeply in his heart and soul that nothing you can do will quench his love for you."

"So this is good-bye."

"Not forever. I am certain we will meet again. I bid you a good day and a safe trip to London."

"I'm not going to London. My next stop is South Hampton."

Olivia turned on her heel and made a quick exit. Whatever the purpose of Olivia's visit, she wasn't about to tell him. Cecil's heart beat with anxiety. Surely Olivia planned to see Eunice. What would she say to her?

twelve

Eunice and her aunt sat together at the empty dining room table. Even though Eunice thought the dinner party was still too far away to take such a step, she and Aunt May had met with the best local caterers, who had left lists of suggested menus. Her aunt was too excited about the prospects to delay discussion.

Eunice picked up several and reviewed them.

"What do you think?" Aunt May prodded. "I like the looks of this one. The main course is rabbit."

Eunice reviewed the selections. Several courses were offered, all sumptuous. Yet the prices were enough to make anyone pale. "These menus will cost us a small fortune. Can Cook prepare a meal that is just as sumptuous for much less?"

Aunt May sent Eunice several quick shakes of her head. "I believe in good stewardship of our resources as much as you do, my dear, but if this is to be our first dinner party since the house renovations, I believe the meal must be one to remember. One that will be talked about for years to come. And that means catered, of course."

"Do I gather that the brigadier general would look most favorably upon a catered affair?"

"Well," she admitted, "if the menu pleases his discerning palate, surely it will please everyone else as well." Point made, Aunt May smiled in triumph, though she set aside the menu including rabbit. "So which do you prefer for our dinner? Roast beef or mutton? Or perhaps both?"

"Whichever you prefer, Auntie." Eunice sighed. She was

aware that her voice held no enthusiasm. But how could she work up any excitement over a dinner? Ever since she stopped seeing Cecil, the days seemed ever so dreary.

"You know, Lord Richard asked about you after Sunday services the other day."

"Do you mean the same gangly Lord Richard with the hooked nose and beady eyes?"

Aunt May sniffed. "I prefer to think of him as a tall gentleman with an aquiline nose and sharp blue eyes."

Blue eyes. But not as blue as Cecil's.

Aunt May peered down her nose at Eunice. "Since when did one's appearance figure so prominently in your judgment?"

"Appearance is only important if one is considering looking at that person every day over breakfast and dinner for the rest of one's life."

"You cannot fool me. I know who you have in mind. If you are thinking that Lord Sutton is the handsomest man the empire has to offer, I think you might need to make use of a good pair of spectacles." Aunt May shook her head. "I fail to see what hold that man has over you."

Eunice laughed. "Oh, Auntie. What is it they say? Beauty is in the eye of the beholder? I have always felt drawn to Cecil with his confident way and his beautiful blue eyes."

"There, there. Please do not drool over the menus. We must return them to the caterers."

"Perhaps they will believe their food evoked such a response."

"And perchance offer us a discount? Flattery will only get you somewhere in the ways of love, not commerce, I am afraid."

At that moment, the butler entered. "Miladies, you have a caller."

"A caller?" Eunice asked. "Is there not a soul in the parish who knows the meaning of *at home*? I thought we made it clear that we receive visitors on Thursday afternoons."

"Yes, you did, milady. Shall I send her away?"

"Her? Of course not," Aunt May answered. "You say it is a woman?"

"Yes, milady. And she is alone."

"Give me her card." After she read the name, a gasp escaped her lips. "Why, Olivia has come to see us!"

Eunice took the card from her aunt and read it. "I would not have thought so had I not seen the card with my own eyes. All the way from London?"

"She will be expecting to stay the night," Aunt May pointed out. "And no doubt, she will make all sorts of demands. She has arrived without any notice whatsoever yet will expect us to treat her as though she were the Prince Regent himself."

Recalling her aunt's demands for her favorite foods when they stayed at Olivia's, Eunice held back a smile. "Then we will just have to try to treat her as though royal blood courses through her veins. And another thing—he shall stay as long as she wishes," Eunice said. "After all, we imposed upon her hospitality on our way here." Eunice nodded to the butler. "Send her into the parlor and have tea prepared immediately."

"Yes, milady."

Aunt May stood up and peered into the mirror. "I must freshen up."

Eunice strode up behind Aunt May and observed her own reflection. "I could use a little freshening myself."

Olivia's voice interrupted. "Whatever for, Eunice? It is just I, your cousin."

"Olivia! We—I—thought you were supposed to be in the parlor."

The butler came up behind her. Exasperation showed on his face. "I beg you pardon, miladies. I instructed her to remain in the parlor, but. . ."

Eunice had no doubt that he spoke the truth. "That is quite

all right. You are excused."

"I did not think you would mind my coming right in to see you," Olivia explained. "After all, we are family."

Eunice nodded. Since she had been expecting no one that day, she was wearing a simple housedress that was flattering in green but slightly out of fashion. Cornered, she had no choice but to recover by pasting a smile on her face and greeting Olivia. "Yes, indeed. How lovely to see you again! And how lovely you look today. All in such a beautiful yellow." Eunice lightly hugged her cousin.

Aunt May followed her example, then broke the embrace. "Yes, you do, my dear. Just like a newly opened daffodil. So now tell us. Whatever are you doing out here? Visiting Lord Sutton, I presume? And you were kind enough to remember to stop by and visit us. How magnificent!"

"Thank you. If you would be so kind, I would welcome a bed for the night."

"But of course," Eunice said. "Stay as long as you like. You were so kind to us in London. The least we can do is to offer you our best hospitality."

Olivia looked around the room. Eunice knew she was appraising the wainscoting that was in dire need of painting and the wallpaper that had seen better days. "Such as it can be, in a house that has been allowed to come to ruin," Olivia remarked.

"We found the house in this condition, regrettably," Eunice hastened to explain.

"Even worse!" Aunt May added.

Eunice cringed at her aunt's honest admission. "Yes, we have done a great deal to improve the place since our arrival."

"Oh, yes," Aunt May agreed. "Have you seen the parlor?"

"No. I heard you instruct the butler to direct me there." Olivia surveyed the worn upholstery on the chairs. "If that is the only room you have been able to pretty up, I understand why."

Eunice decided to ignore Olivia's insult. "Please, allow me to instruct the servants to gather your bags and take them up to my room. You can sleep there tonight."

Olivia raised her eyebrows. "You have no guest room?"

"We have several, oh my, yes," Aunt May said. "But truly, Eunice's is the best room in the house. Except mine, of course."

"I can sleep in a guest room," Eunice said.

Olivia shrugged. "If you insist. Now, what do you plan to serve for dinner? Mutton chops, I hope."

"I think Cook was preparing a vegetable stew," Eunice said.

"Vegetable stew?" Olivia grimaced. "My, but you eat humbly out here in the country. Well, I suppose if that is the best you can do. . ."

"No doubt Cook can find some mutton chops to prepare for dinner tonight," Aunt May said.

Eunice protested, "I am not so sure—"

"Nonsense," Aunt May said. "Our cook is the finest in the parish. Practically a magician."

"I shall see Cook about a change in the menu for this evening," Eunice said.

"Wonderful. Perhaps she can make blood pudding, too."

"I shall inquire." Eunice gritted her teeth. "In the meantime, please do enjoy your tea in the parlor. Why not start without me, Auntie dear? I shall be in soon."

"Oh, I am a bit hungry. I should be delighted to begin," Aunt May said. "Do come along, will you, Olivia?"

"But of course, Aunt May. I could use a little refreshment."

Eunice made a quick exit to the kitchen. After spending a good ten minutes convincing Cook that she could indeed prepare lamb chops in time for dinner—no matter that she had been saving them for Sunday dinner—Eunice looked down at her dress and decided to change into something more suitable for afternoon tea. Olivia could make her feel inferior about her dining-hall decor, but she could no longer poke fun at Eunice's dresses. Not now, given that Eunice had hired the best seamstress in the village to sew her a proper wardrobe.

For this afternoon's tea, she hurriedly chose a white silk dress, which she wore over several muslin underskirts. Lace at the collar called attention to the blond curls around her face and was crocheted in the same pattern as the lace at the hem of her dress. She wore a matching pair of silk slippers, which completed the look. She was ready to face Olivia once again.

"Eunice, dear, you did not need to change your dress just for me," Olivia protested.

"You do look as a vision, like a heavenly white cloud," Aunt May said.

"Indeed," Olivia agreed, her tone begrudging her the compliment. "But my dear, you did not need to dress in your finest."

"Oh, this is not my finest. It is merely the tea gown I wear on many afternoons. So," she hastened to add, "have you seen Cecil yet?"

"Yes."

"I am sure you were quite charmed by Cecilia."

"She is a pretty little girl, though I saw her only briefly. I spoke to your friend, Abigail."

"And how are things at Sutton Manor?" Eunice asked.

"Surely I do not need to tell you. I understand from Giles that you visit at least once a week, ostensibly to give Cecil lessons in etiquette."

"Ostensibly? Indeed not! I have given him lessons that have delivered great benefit. Could you not see his progress for yourself?"

Olivia lifted her nose in the air as though facts forced her to make a concession to Eunice. "Admittedly, I could see a bit of improvement."

"Enough for you to marry him?"

"No."

"No?" Eunice felt her eyes widen in disbelief. "Why, I think he has become the perfect gentleman since he left London. He no longer smokes or consumes hard drink."

"That is not what Giles told me."

"His one setback was Giles's doing. He confessed as much to me himself. I am sure that Cecil has not touched either tobacco or drink since you last saw him."

Olivia looked at the clock on the mantel. "I saw him an hour ago. You must not know Cecil very well."

"How dare you!" Eunice regretted the words as soon as she spoke them.

"How dare I?"

"I am sorry. I never meant to chastise you," Eunice said. "You are my cousin, after all."

"Never mind. I suppose I deserved it." Olivia swallowed her tea. "I deliberately insulted Cecil just to see how you would react. And you responded just as I suspected. You really do love him."

"But Aunt May has forbidden me to see him. And even if she did, it would not matter. He does not love me."

"That is where you are wrong. He does love you. He told me so himself."

Eunice could barely contain herself from leaping off the sofa and dancing around the parlor with joy.

"So that is why you came here? To test Eunice?" Aunt May asked.

"Do I not have a right? After all, she has won his heart, and I have been left out in the cold."

Eunice's joy evaporated. "No! I never meant for that to happen."

"Indeed," Aunt May said. "That is why I forbade her to see

Lord Sutton again. I could see by the look in her eyes that they were becoming too close."

Eunice rushed to Olivia's side and knelt. She took Olivia's hands in her own. "Olivia, I do not want Cecil if it means taking him away from you. Never."

Olivia's face registered shock. "Do you really mean that?"

"With all my heart." Eunice squeezed her cousin's hand. "Please, go to him. Go back to Sutton Manor. Do not waste a moment. Tell him you will marry him today if that is what he wants."

Olivia's jaw slackened. She shook her head. "You really mean what you say."

"Of course I do. I could never be happy if I were the cause of your unhappiness."

"Then you are more of a fool than I thought. What have I done to deserve your consideration?"

"It never was necessary for you to do anything. You are part of my family and one of God's special creations. Is that not enough for me to consider your happiness?"

"I—I do not know what to say."

Eunice could tell that tears threatened to spill down Olivia's cheeks as she rose quickly from her seat, excused herself, and hurried up the stairs. Eunice stood and began to follow.

"No." Aunt May placed a restraining hand on her arm. "Let her alone. She is heartbroken. Can you not see that?"

"How can she be heartbroken? She has just received the most precious gift I can give her."

"On the contrary. I suspect that the gift is no longer yours to give."

❧

Olivia chose to stay only one night, despite their protests that she could stay longer. She was reclusive during the few hours she remained, having breakfast sent to her room. Eunice couldn't blame her cousin for desiring her solitude. Olivia was a proud woman. Admitting defeat could not have come easily for her. After sharing grace over breakfast with Aunt May, Eunice added her own silent prayer.

Father in heaven, I thank Thee for giving Olivia the strong heart and courage to concede that she was not meant for Cecil. I pray for Olivia's happiness, Lord, and for her to draw closer to Thee in her search for peace. In Thy Son's name, amen.

The maid interrupted just as they were about to complete their meal. "Your guest is about to depart, miladies."

"We shall go to the great hall to bid her farewell immediately."

"Yes, milady."

An instant later, they were saying their good-byes.

"I wish you could stay longer," Eunice told Olivia, and she meant it.

Olivia looked through the open front door at the blue sky. A dreamy look covered her expression. "There is nothing here for me. My life is in London."

"Surely there was just a misunderstanding between you and Cecil. If you go to him—"

"No." She shook her head.

"I am so sorry. I never meant to come between you. Please, forgive me."

Olivia faced Eunice. "There is nothing for me to forgive of you. If anything, I should be thanking you. Now I can leave, knowing that Cecil will be well taken care of. . .by you."

Eunice wanted to protest that she didn't want Cecil, but she couldn't. Not without lying. "I cannot." She tilted her head toward Aunt May.

Olivia turned her attention to the older woman. "Aunt May, I implore you not to keep Eunice away from Cecil if he is the one she wants. Let her enjoy the happiness she deserves."

"But can he make her happy?" Aunt May asked. "You know his past."

"His old life is only his past, no longer his present," Olivia said. "I can see how much he has changed."

Eunice remembered one of her favorite passages from the sixth chapter of Romans, " 'Our old man is crucified with him, that the body of sin might be destroyed, that henceforth we should not serve sin.' "

"Yes," Olivia agreed. "I believe that passage does indeed apply to Cecil. Thank you, Eunice, for giving him a better life."

"You are the one who started the process," Eunice pointed out.

"But you are the one who finished it."

"I deserve no credit," Eunice assured her. "The Lord and Savior is responsible for Cecil's change of mind and heart. I was merely His unworthy vessel."

"I do not judge you to be unworthy," Aunt May said. "If anything, Lord Sutton is far beneath you both. But Eunice, if you believe he is the one you want and Olivia has given you her leave, then I will no longer keep you from him."

Eunice took in a happy breath. "Really? Do you mean it, Auntie?" Seeing her aunt's smile, Eunice embraced her.

Aunt May returned the embrace. "My own love was snatched from me by war. I will not let another kind of hate—my distaste for him—keep you apart."

"You will not be around Cecil long before you will grow fond of him, Aunt May. I am sure of it."

"Then I leave Cecil in good hands." Olivia looked pleased. "I wish you the best of luck."

Unwilling to tell Olivia that she didn't believe in luck, Eunice merely nodded her thanks.

After a final embrace, Olivia departed. Eunice watched her make her way to her carriage. She held her head up, as Eunice would have expected of a prideful woman. Yet instead of seeming like a woman defeated, Olivia seemed to Eunice to have more life back in her step.

"Strange. She does not seem so unhappy for a woman who lost her fiancé." Eunice knit her eyebrows together in puzzlement.

"I think she is happy for you and happy that she has gotten back her freedom," Aunt May said.

"But she seemed a bit distraught yesterday."

"Of course she was. No one likes to lose to a rival. Especially an unexpected one."

Eunice didn't need for her aunt to explain further. She knew that Olivia had always considered her a little country mouse, never a threat to her great beauty and sophistication. As the carriage departed, Eunice waved a final farewell to her cousin.

"I would not worry about Olivia," Aunt May consoled her. "She always said she never wanted to marry."

Eunice brought her hand to her side. "Do you think she really means such a thing, Auntie?"

Aunt May nodded. "And so I believe that you have done her—and Lord Sutton—a favor."

In her heart, Eunice knew her aunt spoke the truth. "Now would you do me a favor, Auntie?"

"Of course."

"Would you write a missive to Cecil, granting him permission to see me?"

She hesitated only a moment before nodding her assent. "I never thought I would see the day, but yes, I will write to him this very moment." In keeping with her commitment, she headed to her study.

Her aunt's promise left Eunice with a feeling of such happiness that she wanted to fly. She stepped out into the sunshine, just so she could be closer to the possibility. The sky had never seemed bluer. The sun never shone more brightly. She breathed in a gulp of fresh air. Lifting her arms skyward, she twirled, the bottoms of her pink silk shoes tapping against the ground.

"Eunice!" Aunt May interrupted. "What are you doing? Get back in the house this instant! Do you want to ruin your new slippers?"

"Oh, Auntie! Who cares about slippers?" Eunice took her aunt's hands and tried to convince her, with gentle tugging, into joining her in the joyous dance.

Aunt May pulled her hands out of Eunice's and swatted at her as though she were a pesky fly. "I am long past such frivolity."

"But Auntie, would you say so if the brigadier general were to ask you to dance?"

Aunt May sniffed. "He is much too dignified for such nonsense." She shook her head. "Impetuous child!" She held up the letter she had just written. "I suppose I shall have to find one of the stable boys to deliver this to Sutton Manor."

"Can I not deliver it myself?"

"Child!" Aunt May nearly swooned with horror. "Have you lost all sense of propriety? Of course not."

Eunice wished she could fly the letter to Cecil herself, but she could not. She would have to wait for Cecil's response. She could only pray that the wait would be a short one.

❧

A week went by and still there was no word from Cecil.

"Are you quite sure that the letter was delivered to the estate?" Eunice asked Aunt May over breakfast.

"Yes. Philip told me he delivered the letter himself."

"Oh." Eunice knew disappointment weighed heavily in her voice.

"Do not become discouraged, dear," Aunt May said. "If he is not kind enough to respond to my letter, then he is not the one for you."

Eunice nodded. She knew her aunt was right, but what Aunt May didn't know was how fervently Eunice had been praying that Cecil would visit soon.

"Perhaps you could call on Abigail later this morning?" Aunt May suggested, her tone conspiratorial.

"No, Auntie. I will not create an excuse to see him. He will have to come to me."

Aunt May sighed. "Very well, then."

Eunice searched for a way to take her mind off of Cecil. "The flowers in the great hall need to be refreshed. I think I shall gather a bouquet today."

"A splendid idea. And you might pick a few for your room, too."

"Yes. Nothing is more cheery than flowers."

"I think the lilacs are in bloom. They fill the house with such a lovely fragrance."

"Yes, I quite agree. I shall search for lilacs, then."

Before venturing into the garden, Eunice, with the help of her ladies maid, changed from her morning attire, meant to be worn indoors, to her gardening dress. Green dots decorated the white sleeves and skirt, which were brought together by a green bodice. Three rows of lace decorated the skirt a few inches above the hem, the same lace that could be found on the matching bonnet. Cream-colored, kid leather, half boots protected her feet, clad in white stockings, from any mud she might encounter.

With a reed basket swinging from her arm, Eunice ventured out to the east garden, where she knew she would find plenty of lilacs. Spending time in the garden among the many scented flowers soothed her. Each petal reminded her of

God's tender loving care for His creatures. Not only did He provide delicious vegetables, but He gave the world the flowers that added color for the eye to behold, soft petals for the fingers to touch, scent for the nose to inhale.

She was losing herself in the scent of an especially full lilac bloom when she heard the clomping of a horse's hooves. She turned and saw someone mounted tall and proud upon a fine steed.

Cecil!

Apparently he spotted Eunice, as he directed General to approach the garden. Eunice wanted to run to him as fast as her feet would carry her, but she could not let go of all her dignity. Holding her head up with pride, she meandered toward him.

Judging from the way he leapt off his horse and hastened toward her, his own dignity was the last thing on Cecil's mind.

"Eunice!"

She tried to keep her voice calm, despite her beating heart. "Good morning, Cecil."

Instead of his usual sweet greeting of brushing his lips against her wrist, he chose a more urgent gesture of placing his palms on her forearms. "I rushed here as soon as I received your aunt's letter."

"Rushed? How can you say that?" She raised her eyebrows. "She had it delivered last week."

"I know. At least, I know now. Oh, Eunice, I thought I had lost you."

Eunice was more confused than ever. "Lost me?"

"Yes. Olivia stopped by without warning and demanded that we marry."

"When?" She searched his blue eyes for an answer.

"She wanted us to marry within the month." He tightened his grip on her arms, although his touch remained gentle.

"But I just could not agree to set a date. Not any date. How could I ever marry her when my heart is with you?"

"With me?" Eunice clutched the handle of her basket, then let it drop to her side upon the ground.

Father in heaven, please keep me from fainting dead away with ecstasy!

"She could see, and so could I, that a marriage between us would be an awful mistake. But when she left, she said she was coming here."

"And she did."

"What did she say? She did not do or say anything to hurt you, I pray."

"Of course not. Why, if she had not visited us before she returned to London, Aunt May never would have granted her permission for you to see me. Olivia convinced her that she should not keep us apart." Eunice felt her cheeks grow hot. "I have said too much."

"No, my dear, you have said just enough. I am sorry I did not come here to see you sooner. But you see, I did not receive your letter until just now."

Anger rose to her throat. "Then my stable boy shall be dismissed!"

"Please, do not take such a rash action. Your servant is not to blame. He delivered the missive straight into Tedric's hands. But that morning before the letter was delivered, I was called away on urgent business. I only returned today." He took her hands in his. "During this entire week, in every free moment, I thought of nothing but you."

"And I thought of nothing but you. I was sure you had ignored my aunt's letter. I was certain that your silence meant that you never wanted to see me again."

"But I do. Every day for the rest of my life." Obviously not mindful of how the mud might affect his beige riding pants,

Cecil knelt on one knee before her. He took off his top hat and held it to his chest. With his free hand, he grasped both of hers. "Miss Eunice Norwood, will you do me the great honor of becoming my wife?"

She didn't hesitate. "Yes! Yes! A thousand times, yes!"

Cecil rose to his feet in an instant and took her in his arms. "I trust our experience in this garden will be quite different from our first encounter."

"Indeed."

As his lips touched hers, she dissolved into the moment. The past was but a distant memory. All she cared about was the present and, as she sought the long-awaited pleasure of his lips, the future.

"I never thought I would say this, but I am glad you slapped me silly the first time I tried to kiss you," he said in between kisses.

"Your love has been worth the wait," she whispered.

"I know our match will seem odd, my love," Cecil said between kisses. "We are certain to be called the lady and the cad."

"On the contrary. We shall be the lady and the gentleman, my darling," Eunice replied. "For that is what the Lord has made you—a gentleman in every sense of the word."

A Letter To Our Readers

Dear Reader:

In order that we might better contribute to your reading enjoyment, we would appreciate your taking a few minutes to respond to the following questions. We welcome your comments and read each form and letter we receive. When completed, please return to the following:

Fiction Editor
Heartsong Presents
PO Box 719
Uhrichsville, Ohio 44683

1. Did you enjoy reading *The Lady and the Cad* by Tamela Hancock Murray?
   ❑ Very much! I would like to see more books by this author!
   ❑ Moderately. I would have enjoyed it more if

   _____

   _____

   _____

2. Are you a member of **Heartsong Presents**? ❑ Yes ❑ No
   If no, where did you purchase this book? _____

   _____

3. How would you rate, on a scale from 1 (poor) to 5 (superior), the cover design? _____

4. On a scale from 1 (poor) to 10 (superior), please rate the following elements.

   ____ Heroine   ____ Plot
   ____ Hero   ____ Inspirational theme
   ____ Setting   ____ Secondary characters

5. These characters were special because?_____

_____

_____

6. How has this book inspired your life?_____

_____

_____

7. What settings would you like to see covered in future
   Heartsong Presents books? _____

_____

_____

8. What are some inspirational themes you would like to see
   treated in future books? _____

_____

_____

9. Would you be interested in reading other **Heartsong
   Presents** titles? ❑ Yes ❑ No

10. Please check your age range:

      ❑ Under 18   ❑ 18-24

      ❑ 25-34   ❑ 35-45

      ❑ 46-55   ❑ Over 55

Name_____

Occupation _____

Address _____

City_____ State_____ Zip_____

The STUFF OF LOVE

4 stories in 1

In four interwoven novellas set in 1941, an American OSS officer enlists a mother and daughter in America and two of their relatives in Europe to carry out a clever plan.

The southern California mother/daughter team of Cathy Marie Hake and Kelly Eileen Hake combine their writing and research with authors Sally Laity and Dianna Crawford of northern California.

Historical, paperback, 352 pages, 5 ³/₁₆" x 8"

Heartsong ♥

Presents

___HP496 Meet Me with a Promise, J. A. Grote
___HP499 Her Name Was Rebekah,
          B. K. Graham
___HP500 Great Southland Gold, M. Hawkins
___HP503 Sonoran Secret, N. J. Farrier
___HP504 Mail-Order Husband, D. Mills
___HP507 Trunk of Surprises, D. Hunt
___HP508 Dark Side of the Sun, R. Druten
___HP511 To Walk in Sunshine, S. Laity
___HP512 Precious Burdens, C. M. Hake
___HP515 Love Almost Lost, I. B. Brand
___HP516 Lucy's Quilt, J. Livingston
___HP519 Red River Bride, C. Coble
___HP520 The Flame Within, P. Griffin
___HP523 Raining Fire, L. A. Coleman
___HP524 Laney's Kiss, T. V. Bateman
___HP531 Lizzie, L. Ford
___HP532 A Promise Made, J. L. Barton
___HP535 Viking Honor, D. Mindrup
___HP536 Emily's Place, T. V. Bateman
___HP539 Two Hearts Wait, F. Chrisman
___HP540 Double Exposure, S. Laity
___HP543 Cora, M. Colvin
___HP544 A Light Among Shadows, T. H. Murray
___HP547 Maryelle, L. Ford
___HP548 His Brother's Bride, D. Hunter
___HP551 Healing Heart, R. Druten
___HP552 The Vicar's Daughter, K. Comeaux
___HP555 But For Grace, T. V. Bateman

___HP556 Red Hills Stranger, M. G. Chapman
___HP559 Banjo's New Song, R. Dow
___HP560 Heart Appearances, P. Griffin
___HP563 Redeemed Hearts, C. M. Hake
___HP564 Tender Hearts, K. Dykes
___HP567 Summer Dream, M. H. Flinkman
___HP568 Loveswept, T. H. Murray
___HP571 Bayou Fever, K. Y'Barbo
___HP572 Temporary Husband, D. Mills
___HP575 Kelly's Chance, W. E. Brunstetter
___HP576 Letters from the Enemy, S. M. Warren
___HP579 Grace, L. Ford
___HP580 Land of Promise, C. Cox
___HP583 Ramshakle Rose, C. M. Hake
___HP584 His Brother's Castoff, L. N. Dooley
___HP587 Lilly's Dream, P. Darty
___HP588 Torey's Prayer, T. V. Bateman
___HP591 Eliza, M. Colvin
___HP592 Refining Fire, C. Cox
___HP595 Surrendered Heart, J. Odell
___HP596 Kiowa Husband, D. Mills
___HP599 Double Deception, L. Nelson Dooley
___HP600 The Restoration, C. M. Hake
___HP603 A Whale of a Marriage, D. Hunt
___HP604 Irene, L. Ford
___HP607 Protecting Amy, S. P. Davis
___HP608 The Engagement, K. Comeaux
___HP611 Faithful Traitor, J. Stengl
___HP612 Michaela's Choice, L. Harris

Great Inspirational Romance at a Great Price!

Heartsong Presents books are inspirational romances in contemporary and historical settings, designed to give you an enjoyable, spirit-lifting reading experience. You can choose wonderfully written titles from some of today's best authors like Peggy Darty, Sally Laity, Tracie Peterson, Colleen L. Reece, Debra White Smith, and many others.

When ordering quantities less than twelve, above titles are $2.97 each.
Not all titles may be available at time of order.

$\mathcal{H}$EARTSONG ❤ PRESENTS
Love Stories
Are Rated G!

That's for godly, gratifying, and of course, great! If you love a thrilling love story but don't appreciate the sordidness of some popular paperback romances, **Heartsong Presents** is for you. In fact, **Heartsong Presents** is the premiere inspirational romance book club featuring love stories where Christian faith is the primary ingredient in a marriage relationship.

Sign up today to receive your first set of four, never-before-published Christian romances. Send no money now; you will receive a bill with the first shipment. You may cancel at any time without obligation, and if you aren't completely satisfied with any selection, you may return the books for an immediate refund!

Imagine. . .four new romances every four weeks—two historical, two contemporary—with men and women like you who long to meet the one God has chosen as the love of their lives. . .all for the low price of $10.99 postpaid.

To join, simply complete the coupon below and mail to the address provided. **Heartsong Presents** romances are rated G for another reason: They'll arrive Godspeed!

YES! Sign me up for Hearts❤ng!

NEW MEMBERSHIPS WILL BE SHIPPED IMMEDIATELY!
Send no money now. We'll bill you only $10.99 post-paid with your first shipment of four books. Or for faster action, call toll free 1-800-847-8270.

NAME _____

ADDRESS _____

CITY _____ STATE _____ ZIP _____

MAIL TO: HEARTSONG PRESENTS, P.O. Box 721, Uhrichsville, Ohio 44683
or visit www.heartsongpresents.com